PRODIGAL KISS
(a play with songs)

[inspired by Federico Garcia Lorca's *Poet in New York*]

And

PERDITA GRACIA
(A play with songs)

[inspired by Shakespeare's *The Winter's Tale*]

By

Caridad Svich

Lizard Run Press

Isbn: 978-0-578-03671-7

1

Lizard Run Press
Theatre & Performance Texts

New edition 2009 by Lizard Run Press
(an imprint of NoPassport)
PO Box 1786, South Gate, CA 90280 USA; -
NoPassportPress@aol.com
ISBN: 978-0-578-03671-7; $20.00

Lizard Run Press is a boutique imprint of theatre alliance NoPassport devoted to diversity, difference and freedom of expression in the arts with an emphasis on the embrace of the hemispheric spirit.

CONTENTS

Embracing the Fragile

To construct a play, you have to construct multiple identities. You are constantly fragmenting selves and putting them back together again, examining shapes and destroying them: the game of playwriting is centered to a large degree around the task of making and un-making, and making again. The activity demands a strong will, complete faith in the doing, and at the same time it asks that you embrace with every fiber of your artistic being the most fragile part of yourself, for it is that which causes the most exposure, pain, joy, fear, and shame, that will ultimately center the work.

A dear collaborator recently told me that an undeniable, necessary aspect of an artist's maturation process involves "embracing the facile." Not shying away from it or being fearful of it, but taking it in both hands, fully into the body, and using the facility to see yourself through it toward a new phase in your growth.

Without this embrace of your own skill and craftsmanship, you remain in a possibly dishonest place in relationship to your work, and even with the best of intentions, wreck your craft.

Facile. Fragile. Words balanced against each other. I toss them around in my brain as I write. Seventeen years since writing my first "official" play, it has come down to two words and a test of faith. I feel myself in a changed place. Facility is not an enemy, nor my armor, but rather a tool of my trade. A signifier of a certain level of confidence that has come from working diligently at my craft. "Facile" as in at-the-ready with the writing toolbox not outside my body, but in: embodied. Fragility is what I seek when I write. The moment when something is stripped down, bare, to the essence, made vulnerable, and thus, strong. "Fragility" not as in weakness, but as in the tenderest expression – even if it be a brutal one. The moment when everything in a character, a scene, a line, an image could break, and your whole body as receiver of that character, scene, line, image shivers. I look for the shivers when I write. I call it "the fragile." And I use my newly-discovered facility to do so.

But even with twenty years of experience and writing in my pocket, and over twenty theatre pieces to my name, the construction not of my characters' identities, but of own, still comes into play. As a playwright labeled a "Latina" I have been wrestling with the making of an identity I have never really felt my own. With each play I write I feel less and less Latina, and at the same time, more and more Latina. In other words, I feel more and more comfortable in my skin simply as an American writer, which is what I have always been, and thus my cultural heritage is embodied more and more in who I am and what I write.

I do not feel the constant need to define myself for others' eyes, because I am already defined. Ambiguity, thus, can be released into the writing, in the play of moments, feelings, situations that make up the dance of a play. Yet, I know my degree of "Latina-ness" in relationship to other writers is often questioned because of the nature of my writing, its subject matter, the choices that I make when I face the page and let fragility guide me.

Without necessarily convenient signifiers in the work for critics or scholars to identify, the nature of my Latina-ness becomes a sub-topic when discussions of my writing come up. If I am in the room, I feel I have to defend my work and the place from which it springs. The freedom to write is one of the sheer joys of writing. You can indeed be anyone, anything, live anywhere, enact the most outrageous scenarios…nothing except your own talent or imagination can stop you. I certainly don't feel a need to fit into a category because I simply do not believe in them. Categories box things in, make them safe. You can handle something easily if it's in a category, because the words are made available to you, the vocabulary comes pre-packaged. But if the work falls outside categories, or straddles them (as my plays tend to do) then you have to find the words to describe the work, take your time, and try to understand in a different way how the work behaves, or "misbehaves," according to societal rules.

I say this because as a playwright, there is a profound difference between the making of the work and its reception. If indeed I am in the fragile place where my characters send me a shiver and so the work grows – as it has done in plays like *Any Place But Here, Alchemy of Desire/Dead-Man's Blues, Fugitive Pieces, Iphigenia Crash Land Falls on the Neon Shell That Was Once Her Heart, Thrush,* and others – I can only be truthful to that shiver, that moment and use my facility as a writer to
make that truthful moment as alive as I possibly can on the page, which will later be performance. When I am placed in the position of viewing the work, or talking about it, especially in the context of "what does it mean to be a Latina writer in the United States?" then the act of misbehaving becomes the subtext wherein the question is asked of me. And I find myself having to justify why I wrote a character named Simone who happens to live in the South and speaks with a Southern cadence in *Alchemy of Desire* or why the characters of Chucky and Lydia feel so Northeastern in *Any Place But Here,* and it is then

when I resent the reductive nature of how an artist is often called upon to describe the work, if they happen to have been born into an "other" majority.

The resentment, thankfully, subsides or I would not be able to write. But the wrestling with the question of "what makes a work Latina or not?" nags at the back of the mind. Certainly one of the reasons why the anthology *Out of the Fringe: Contemporary Latina/o Theatre and Performance* (which I co-edited with Maria Teresa Merraro) is shaped in the way that it is is because of a desire on my part to upend some of the expected notions of what constitutes "being a Latina/o," and to also have this work be part of a larger, more inclusive discourse in American and world theater.

Oddly enough, the other battle that is still being waged is "what makes a work female or not?" Just a month ago, a colleague who only had read my work, assumed, and with great authority, that I was indeed a male writer. And the reason for this assumption? The violence in my writing.

I have never shied away from the violent nature of my work. Humor and violence have always come hand in hand in my writing. They were a given from the moment I wrote my first story. My fascination with our savage natures comes from a deeply compassionate place, from a generous one.

Not out of indulgence or morbidity. In the theatre there is a long and rich legacy of violence and its examination. The Greeks, Shakespeare, Garcia Lorca, Beckett, Pinter… because of its heightened nature, the public platform which theatre offers allows a writer to confront the dark and sinister in a manner that can be strangely exalting.

Violence is about extremity, and the irrational. Theatre thrives on both. And both offer opportunities to explore the opposite: absolute tenderness, and lucidity. This double effect is what I often am after in the writing. They are the fragile ends that I hold onto as characters shape themselves and re-shape themselves during the course of a play.

The intersection of identities, the dis-equilibrium of moments, is what fascinates me, in part, when I write. Reminding myself of the fragile nature of being human in this peculiar world is the one thing that is constant in the day-to-day process of making my art. Everything else, and I truly mean everything else, falls away in that reminder. Is it more dangerous to speak your mind, or to speak your heart?

This essay was originally written for and published in a special issue of OLLANTAY Theater Magazine devoted to Latina theatre and performance.

PRODIGAL KISS

A play with songs

This play is previously published in
Best New Plays by New Playwrights of 1999
(Smith & Kraus Publishers, Inc., Spring 2001)

Introduction

Migration has always been a central motif in my work. Characters are always leaving one place and finding themselves in another. Destinations are way-laid, and bodies are reborn in new landscapes. *Prodigal Kiss* is my way of looking at the US as if I was born elsewhere. It tracks places that are a strong part of my personal nomadic history, but also lifts those places into an imaginative realm which is purely speculative.

This is a story of a pilgrimage, and as such it offers a spiritual journey into the heart of a young woman who must find a new emotional identity for herself in a new country, but who must also come to terms with an identity she wished to leave behind. Cuba and the US provide the central dynamic for the play's mythos.

The island meets the continent. Spanish and English mix and merge as different characters from the Americas cut their own linguistic paths in an effort to survive. Marcela, the woman at the center of this play, is in transit. Part of her is in Cuba, part of her in the US. This play is an exploration of the split in her soul.

PRODIGAL KISS

A play with songs by Caridad Svich

This play was initially developed with support from the NEA/TCG Playwriting Residency Program at the Mark Taper Forum Theatre in Los Angeles. While in progress, the play received readings at the Traverse Theatre in Edinburgh, Mark Taper Forum Theatre New Work Festival in Los Angeles, New Georges Theatre in New York City, and the King's Head Theatre in London.

A significant part of this play's development is due to a workshop at the Playwrights' Center of Minneapolis' PlayLabs in the summer of 1999 directed by Neel Keller, wherein Anne Garcia Romero served as dramaturg and actors Julie Briskman-Hall, Bill Corbett, J.D. Cutler, and Camille D'Ambrose gave of their talent, humor and generosity.

The play was presented at the Key West Theatre Festival in Key West, Florida (Joan McGillis, Artistic Director) on October 8, 1999. It was directed by Ellen Davis; the set/lighting design was by Gary Macdonald; the costume design was by Ellis Tillman; and the stage manager was Kathleen Balsemo. The cast was as follows:

MARCELA: Delma Miranda

IGNACIO/RAFAEL/PACO: Steve Wise

CORAL/WOMAN ON ROAD/MIRIAM MOCHA: Judith Delgado

RIDER/CARLO/HALF-DRESSED MAN:. Oscar Issac

Special thanks to

Todd Cerveris, Marissa Chibas, Jorge Ignacio Cortinas,
Maria Delgado, John Diehl, Roger Ellis, Julie Briskman-Hall, Philip Howard, Dina Elisa Ibrahim, O-Lan Jones, Neel Keller, Fran Kumin, Megan Monaghan, Anne Garcia Romero, Barry Sherman, Tori Haring-Smith, Ella Wildridge, and Elizabeth Wong

As always, this is for my parents

PRODIGAL KISS

A play with songs by Caridad Svich

Characters:

MARCELA, a woman in her late 20s-early 30s. Open, perseverant.

IGNACIO/RAFAEL/PACO
A man in his early 40s. Sunburnt, sullen/ A man in his 40s. Quick-tempered, pragmatic/ A man in his 30s, Fresh off the boat.

CORAL/WOMAN ON ROAD/MIRIAM MOCHA
A woman in her 70s. Youthful, sly. A survivor/ A vision/ A woman in her 30s. Direct, a bit fanciful.

RIDER/HALf-DRESSED MAN/CARLO
A man in his 20s. nervy, raw/ A john/ A man in his early 30s. Curious, gentle.

Notes:

This play should be performed with an interval after Part One.

The characters in this piece speak an English occasionally peppered with Spanish words and phrases, most of which are translated by them directly, or can be determined from context.

No attempt should be made to have the characters speak with "Hispanic" accents.

The author's original songs featured in the text may be performed a cappella.

Part One: Passage

Scene one
Invocation: Santiago

{MARCELA is standing on a slim board in the middle of the ocean. She begins to sing in Spanish.}

MARCELA
Me voy pa Santiago.
Pa Santiago me voy.
I'm going to Santiago.
To Santiago I go.

Cause I don't want to be here
In this country
I don't want to be here
In this city,
In these mountains
In this land I don't know.

I'm going to Santiago.
To Cuba I go.
Back to Santiago.
The land I call home.

{breath}

A sky of silver
Hangs over a tobacco slum.
I dream of Santiago

And a child drowning in the sun.

With copper coins in the mouth
And hot ferns beating.
Cigar paper hands
That won't stop bleeding.
I dream of Santiago
And its trembling shore,
Under an umbrella of stars
That leaves me hungry for more.

{breath}

On a dark ocean
Beneath the moon's glow,
The lights of Santiago
Call me back home.

But I cannot go back
To my country.
No. I cannot go back
To my city,
To my sierra,
To the land that I know.

I dream of Santiago
As it fades into the void.
On a boat of black water,
Let my heart be destroyed.

{A shivering of stars. Dark.}

Scene two

{A road by a field of saw-grass. MARCELA is standing with an old brown suitcase in hand, looking out. IGNACIO appears from the saw grass. In his hand, a small paper bag. He is poorly clothed and uncomfortably sunburnt. He looks at MARCELA.}

IGNACIO: Where are you from?

MARCELA: Santiago.

IGNACIO: Which one?

MARCELA: Eh?

IGNACIO: There are six of them, if you count San Diego.

MARCELA: …Cuba.

IGNACIO: I'm from Spain.

MARCELA: Yes?

IGNACIO: Santiago de Compostela. The road to Saint James.

MARCELA: Saint James? I saw his statue –

IGNACIO: Down a stretch?

MARCELA: When I got off the boat. Yes. I saw it and I thought, "I'll be protected here."

IGNACIO: You ever been?

MARCELA: What?

IGNACIO: To Santiago de Compostela?

MARCELA: No.

IGNACIO: You should go. It's where everything ends.

MARCELA: What do you mean?

IGNACIO: It's the last Santiago after all the Santiagos, the last star on the map.

MARCELA: Last star?

IGNACIO: All roads lead to Saint James. That's why people go to my Santiago. Flocks and flocks of mad pilgrims seeking to be blessed by Saint James' hand, seeking to be healed, so they can put a part of their lives behind and spend the rest of their time in grace.

MARCELA: I'd like that.

IGNACIO: Just follow the stars of the Milky Way straight to "Finisterre." You ever heard Santiago de Compostela called that name?

MARCELA: Not that I...

IGNACIO: "Fi-nis-terre." End of the world.

MARCELA: *(to herself)* Finisterre.

IGNACIO: It's the last place on earth before you reach heaven. That's what the ancients believed about my Santiago.

MARCELA: Is that what you believe?

IGNACIO: I was born there. I believe a bit of everything.

{Pause.}

My name's Ignacio. I come on the bus. You?

MARCELA: Marcela. Boat.

IGNACIO: Sailboat?

MARCELA: Of a kind.

IGNACIO: Long ride…

MARCELA: Hmm?

IGNACIO: …I had me a long ride on the bus. It stops by every couple of hours or so off the road a dozen miles back.

MARCELA: Oh.

IGNACIO: It won't do you any good to wait here. You want the bus, you got to walk. Won't be a car come down this road for hours, if that's what you're thinking.

MARCELA: I'm not thinking of anything. I'm looking at the grass. Never seen…

IGNACIO: Saw grass. It grows so tall and wild down here in Florida, they got it mow it down every hour or so.

MARCELA: Makes me dizzy just to look at it.

IGNACIO: How's that?

MARCELA: It's like a green bonfire. I bet if I put my hand to it, it would holler with promise.

IGNACIO: The leaves will assassinate you if you brush against them too hard.

MARCELA: How's that?

IGNACIO: They don't call it "saw-grass" for nothing.

{IGNACIO opens paper bag, revealing a bottle of wine that opens by unscrewing the cap.}

Drink?

MARCELA: No.

IGNACIO: I stole this from a shop. Sweet dessert wine from Malaga. Have you been there?

MARCELA: No.

IGNACIO: Down near Morocco. Hundreds of miles from my Santiago. *{sings}* *"Malaga, Malaga. Las ninas cantan en Malaga..."*
Cheap rotten wine, but sweet. Sweet enough to give you a spit rush. You sure you don't want some?

MARCELA: I'm sure.

IGNACIO: So, where are you headed? You can't look at the grass all day.

MARCELA: I just want to set my eyes beyond the equator. Past trees, sand, gray-green rivers, aching moons, curving waters, and burning yolks of light.

IGNACIO: Past Cuba, eh?

MARCELA: Past everything. Start new.

IGNACIO: With saw grass?

MARCELA: Whatever comes to me. Let my eyes cast down on wheat fields and deserts, And tall buildings that reach into infinity, and red mountains that will take my breath and just split it into a hundred million pieces, because that's what beauty can do. It can change you.

IGNACIO: Not too close now.

MARCELA: What?

IGNACIO: The saw grass will cut you to slivers if you run through it. ...If you want to go anywhere, you'll need a ticket.

MARCELA: What?

IGNACIO: From the kiosk.

MARCELA: Kiosk?

IGNACIO: Shack, stand, booth. A place where you get a ticket.

MARCELA: I understand.

IGNACIO: See, you got to have a record of where you've been, where you're going.
If you don't, nobody believes you. They think you haven't been anywhere except where you're from. And I'm not from damn Spain anymore. *Joder*. Not with everywhere I've been. But I don't show a ticket, who's to say?
I could be lunching on death like a town drunk carrying nothing more than a night's skeleton on my tongue. Drink?

MARCELA: No.

IGNACIO: You cut cross oceans and borders to come here, but the only way you'll get to see the whole country is with a ticket in hand.

MARCELA: I don't know about the whole country –

IGNACIO: I've seen every goddamn inch of it.

MARCELA: Have you been to New Jersey?
My aunt lives in New Jersey.

{*MARCELA reaches into her bra.*}

IGNACIO: Hold on, hold on now.

MARCELA: What?

IGNACIO: I don't want to…

MARCELA: What are you talking about? It's
just a letter she wrote.

{*MARCELA pulls out a folded piece of paper from
her bra.*}

She writes about so many things, things you
can't even dream: Shelves and shelves of food,
fields of corn, sunflowers that rise up to the
sky.

IGNACIO: Sunflowers, eh?

MARCELA: Straight up. Like giant angels.
And thick twigs and pine –

IGNACIO: Nothing like your burnt-out cane
fields, eh?

MARCELA: Would you like to read it?

IGNACIO: …You know what the pilgrims used to do back when I was in Santiago de Compostela? They would carry around signs, scribbled-down notes about where they'd been.Every time they would reach a turn in the road, they'd pin a note to their back, so you could tell the truly mad pilgrims by how many pieces of paper they had down their spine. I used to throw rocks at them, one rock per paper, to see if they would stop, If they would give up on Saint James, cause the dead bastard couldn't do anything for them anyway.
One time I threw a hundred rocks at this man. One… But he just kept going, *hijo de puta*, he wouldn't stop, Even though he had blood down his back. I don't read letters. I don't want signs. I got enough with a ticket.

{MARCELA slips letter back in her bra.}

MARCELA: You haven't been to New Jersey.

IGNACIO: I've stretched myself along a good half of Canada, partway down Mexico.
I got myself caught a couple of times. They said they'd ship me back from where I came. I thought, "I'm not going back to Santiago." I mean, you wouldn't go back, would you?

MARCELA: To Cuba? I've nothing to go back to.

IGNACIO: Exactly. So, I got me a ticket. Only thing is, a ticket can run you a good fifty coin and change.

MARCELA: Fifty?

IGNACIO: That too much for you? There's a way around it. There always is. You can get anything you want around here as long as you keep your mouth shut, your pocket sewed tight, and the bottom of your belly dry as a lemon. Bus, train, any way you go. And you want to go, don't you? You want to go somewhere? Where do you want to go?

MARCELA: Kansas. Chicago. St. Louie. New York. New Orleans. Nebraska. Wyoming. The Gulf.

IGNACIO: You'll need a ticket. You'll need to wait at a stop. Past some lights, up the street. You know where I mean?

MARCELA: A kiosk.

IGNACIO: Where the girls piss.

MARCELA: Eh?

IGNACIO: Behind the kiosk. The girls lift their skirts and piss against the wall. In ripe daylight. Like nothing. Like children in a village.

MARCELA: You've seen them?

IGNACIO: I watch them.

MARCELA: You watch them piss?

IGNACIO: I'm not ashamed of it. I watch them through the thistledown. They come down the street, go behind the kiosk, and lift their skirts, flashing their tender asses in the air. Then they piss against the wall, giggle, and lift their arms above their heads. And for a moment, I think they will remain like this - Pantless, fresh, smelling of orange blossoms and violet water. Like children. Yes. – But then they push their skirts down with firm strokes over their thighs, And their giggles become rough, and their hands turn vulgar, and I let out a sigh. And I think "Poor girls in their yellow skirts stinking of newborn piss. How careless they have become. How treacherous of innocence."
And I turn my eyes, as they walk, no more than a glimpse, and watch them go past the boys, who stand in the bare sun wearing leather jackets and mesh tops, boys, who think

nothing of the girls, nothing at all, despite their long, open strides. All the boys want to do is look at each other. *Maricon.* You know what I mean? I make me a some-time living with their kind. Fifty a pop and no questions.

MARCELA: Fifty?

IGNACIO: Straight hustle. Bite and go.

MARCELA: But you look at the girls.

IGNACIO: I watch them. Yes. They remind me of the girls in my village. Like you.

MARCELA: I don't lift my skirt.

IGNACIO: But you piss, don't you?

MARCELA: We all piss.

IGNACIO: But not against the wall. Not so everyone will see. *Putas.* You know what I mean.

MARCELA: Are you calling me a *puta*?
In Cuba, there's a saying –

IGNACIO: In Spain, there's a saying too. But we're not there anymore. This is a whole new land you've come to. We're all the same – rich, poor, and in-between. Whores. That's all we are.

MARCELA: You're wrong.

IGNACIO: Yeah? How'd you get here?
You came on a boat, right? A rubber-and-tin number strapped to the currents of the sea? How'd you get on that boat, Marcela? What did you do? Plead?

MARCELA: Where'd you say this kiosk was?

IGNACIO: *{Continuing}* Or did you suck some gracious wind, suck some air, so you'd be let be?

MARCELA: There were five of us.
A plumber, a factory worker, a mother,
 her child and myself.
No one else. Only sea and sky.
We had food and water for two days.
All we had for power was oars.
 We took turns rowing.
We would row for eight hours and stop.
If we were lucky, a current would catch us
and we could rest our arms.
After two days, there was only a bit of water
left – drinking water, that is –
and we hadn't spotted a plane of fishing boat
anywhere that could save us.

So we bobbed in the waves, tired of rowing,
and watched the sharks swim past.
We started praying.

The child fed on his mother's dry tit,
 and the plumber screamed.
He screamed of fire, snow,
and of a head full of shit.
He screamed so much
 he couldn't get a word out.
After a while, his eyes became fixed. Like glass.
He was staring. At nothing.
But he was still alive.

The factory worker grabbed the child
and began to strangle it with his large hands.
The mother looked at him
with a half-bent smile,
 and offered the factory worker her tit to suck.
The plumber kept staring.
I looked at the sky.

It was of a deep, penetrating blue.
And as it grew dark,
I thought I could see five moons
 lit up at different points in the sky,
 creating a path of light.
And I thought of my Santiago,
 and how it would shine at night –
{Half-sung} "Me voy pa Santiago.
 Pa Santiago me voy…"

The sky turned black. For an instant.
And the boat swayed.
I looked up again at the sky.
I looked for a plane that would see us and not
take aim, as we kept bobbing in the waves.
But there was nothing. Only sky.

And I began to cast my eyes down,
As the factory worker
tied the mother's mouth with kisses,
while the child hung between them like a doll
grown limp and forgotten.
The plumber stared, and kept staring.
His eyes were now fixed on my suitcase.
I could feel the plywood and ropes
tying this mess of a boat give out
 under the weight of the sea.
And that's when he fell, the staring man,
straight into the water, straight down.
And we all looked up. For a moment.
Catching our breath
 as the wind spit on the breeze.

The factory worker let go of the mother,
 and started cursing
 "Cono carajo mierda. Cono carajo. Cono carajo."
The mother looked at me.
She clutched my arm,
digging her nails into my skin,
the dead child between us.
I couldn't move. I couldn't think.

I could only look up. And keep looking.
And just as my eyes were beginning to burn
from the heat of the sun
and the sting of the air,
I saw a plane. A small plane
 flying out from under some wrecking clouds.
And I waved with my free arm,
and yelled with my harsh throat.
And then we all started waving.
Like featherless birds.
Waving and yelling with our mouths
dry as rags, and our brains drunk from the sun
"Bread. Ice. Santiago…"
The plane touched close. Hot metal.
And slowly it lifted us up
into the chill of the air.
And we trembled. And held our breath.
And kissed, kissed all that was alive in us.

And it was then that I felt
I could really look straight ahead without fear
of what would find me,
For I was safe in the belly of that plane.
And I knew earth's will had been done.
Whatever else would come to me,
I would no longer be
at the water's torturous mercy.

IGNACIO: …You had to get on that slip-ass
boat somehow.

MARCELA: I did nothing except run, and throw every last coin I had into buying lumber for that damn boat.

IGNACIO: So, it was money that saved you from whoring.

MARCELA: Not much.

IGNACIO: Enough to buy plywood.

MARCELA: Not enough to get by.

IGNACIO: And what did the factory worker, who surely had not earned a day's pay in quite some time, think of this? What did he think of your bullying generosity as you ran with your fresh-cut plywood to his sorry bit of a boat? Did he want to grab the ass that smelled of hard cash, or did you make him lick it? *Golfa?*Or should I say *jinetera?*

{MARCELA slaps IGNACIO.}

Sharp hand. Sharp as saw grass.

MARCELA: It was all the money I had.

IGNACIO: Money from whom? A Dutchman, or was he Italian? What'd you say? "Give me a dollar and I'll kiss you?"

MARCELA: You don't know what you're talking about.

IGNACIO: Damn *jineteras* always find a way around.

MARCELA: I told you. I am not a *jinetera*. Christ. You haven't listened to a thing I've said.

IGNACIO: I heard everything you didn't say.

MARCELA: You read minds?

IGNACIO: No. But I hear things. Right under the voice, in the back of the tongue, in the intake of breath when something's not spoken.

MARCELA: And what is it you hear?

IGNACIO: Ballads of war. Whispering veins. The hollow song of a girl with coins and baby in her belly –

MARCELA: Stop.

IGNACIO: A girl looking to swim out from under the humid earth of the bitter tropics so she can wander through ports, taverns and dim-lit gardens with new undergarments, free from the clutches of sour men with plastic roses and the taste of grapefruit in their mouths

MARCELA: *{To herself}* Free. Yes.

IGNACIO: Men that tug at her belly and scratch at her breasts until all she has left is a bit of coconut milk on her chin, white seeds from a misplaced equator.

MARCELA: It wasn't like that.

IGNACIO: And so she becomes sick, this girl with hollow veins and the blush of born fruit on her skin. She becomes sick of eating plastic roses, and silver whiskey and hardened gin. And she swims. She swims out and smuggles herself on a rowboat

MARCELA: A board in the middle of the sea

IGNACIO: She pretends she seeks something more noble than a walk in the park, an evening on a bridge, unfettered moments whose equilibrium could break the whole sky, if she were to shout it, if she were to shout what kind of freedom she dreams

MARCELA: *{To herself}* Free of everything, everyone…

IGNACIO: But she keeps quiet, and slips in on a shipwreck of blood

MARCELA: *{To herself}* The staring man fell into the belly of a shark.

IGNACIO: And she steps from water onto land, with her heels high and her bottom clean, lest she be discovered by the shadow of a bird craning its neck over her brown valise. And Saint James, oh Saint James looks on. His statue tall, pleased. He is your guardian as you stand on the road, on the street, catching your face in the shard of a mirror at your feet. He is your guardian because that is his calling – to watch over wayward pilgrims – but not because he feels anything. …The voices of the dead can be heard in this saw grass,
but also those of the living, and what curses they speak. …I know everything there is to know about a girl with coins and a baby in her belly –

MARCELA: I don't have a baby in my belly.

IGNACIO: But you did. Once. I can see the outline of his body through the faint stretch of your skin.

MARCELA: You don't know anything.

IGNACIO: I know you got on that boat, and now you are here, when there are five hundred, thousand others who can't even make it near.

MARCELA: What about you?

IGNACIO: I've always been a whore. That's clear. I've never had to jockey my way to get anywhere. It's always been straight hustle for me: box or dagger. But you. You are some kind of liar, some kind of political meat.

{MARCELA starts to walk away, suitcase in hand.}

Where are you going?

MARCELA: I didn't come all the way here just to look at saw grass.

IGNACIO: But it's beautiful. You said it yourself.

MARCELA: I'm going up the street.

IGNACIO: Up the street?

MARCELA: To the kiosk. "Past some lights." Isn't that what you said?

IGNACIO: I've been so many places. Damned if I know… lights?

MARCELA: I'll find it.

IGNACIO: Hold on now. HOLD ON.

{IGNACIO grabs her.}

MARCELA: What? What do you want?

IGNACIO: I want to hold onto you a bit. You might bring me luck. Luck lies flat on this land, flat on its back. When you got a chance to get hold of it, you got to do it.

MARCELA: What are you -?

IGNACIO: You think I like having to walk miles of road in the sun cause all I got is the bus to drop me wherever it is I want to go? I'd like nothing more than to set down, get me a little juice for my time in this land. And when I came upon you I thought, "Well, this could be my luck, my real live ticket."

MARCELA: Let go.

IGNACIO: Got that brown suitcase. Those eyes.

MARCELA: You want the case? Take the goddamn case.

IGNACIO: What's a beat-up old case going to do for me? No. You got to lift up your skirt. Way up above your head. You got a fine piece of ass here. You got to use it.

MARCELA: Ignacio!

IGNACIO: Ain't no one going to be exempt.

MARCELA: I need a drink.

IGNACIO: What?

MARCELA: Wine. I need some wine.

IGNACIO: Sweet dessert wine?

MARCELA: Yes.

IGNACIO: I wouldn't mind ramming you up from behind with the taste of that sweet wine in your mouth. The girls in Malaga got the best touch when they're tanked up.

{He lets go of her, goes to pick up bottle of wine that is on the ground.}

{sings} *"Malaga. Malaga. Las ninas follan en Malaga…"*

{MARCELA grabs suitcase, goes to hit him with it.}

What are you -?

MARCELA: Get away.

IGNACIO: You're going to hit me with that case?

MARCELA: Get away from me.

IGNACIO: Where am I going to go? We're on a road in the middle of nothing next to a goddamn field of saw-grass.

{MARCELA hits him with case.}

IGNACIO: What the -?

MARCELA: Where is it?

IGNACIO: You want to play rough? Eh? Is that the kind of game you *putas* play down there in Cuba?

MARCELA: The KIOSK. Where is it?

IGNACIO: Up the crossroads, past some lights.

{MARCELA slams him with the case. IGNACIO falls.}

IGNACIO: Co~no…

MARCELA: That's right. *Co~no. C~ono, carajo y mierda.* What the hell do you think you're doing going around trying to stick your cock in everybody's face? Whether they want you to or not? What do you think I am? Huh? What the fuck do you think I am?

{She hits him with case again.}

And don't think I don't know that you're awake. Cause you are plenty awake, *cabron.* You are awake and living in America thinking you can fuck me over cause I just got off the boat. Well, let me tell you: I got some soil here, I got some soil in here that's got nothing to do with you.

{MARCELA opens the case. It is full of dirt. She pours it onto IGNACIO.}

Feel it? This is Cuba. This is that sweet Caribbean ass you want to fuck. You want to taste it? Here.

{MARCELA takes some dirt, grabs him by the hair, lifts his head, and rubs his mouth with the dirt.}

This is what it tastes like. This is what your rum-and-sugar dream taste like, *cabron. {indicating dirt}* Go on now. Swallow. Swallow!

{He swallows the dirt.}

You want to talk to me now? You want to tell me all you know about what you heard and what you didn't hear in that boozed-up head of yours? You are nothing. And I am nothing more than what I aim to be, which is as far from you as I can get in this world. I didn't come here for this. You hear me? I didn't come here through black water and a sky smashed to bits to drown in some sunburnt ash of a man who's got nothing on his mind except leaving fucked-up bodies by the side of the road.

{She dumps all the dirt onto him.}

Here. Bury yourself in it. Think of Spain. Cause there isn't a bus or train that can save you. Not even Saint James can save you now.

{MARCELA throws empty case down. Pause. She looks out.}

To the crossroads. The traffic lights. Up the street.

{MARCELA exits. After a moment, IGNACIO rises.}

Scene three

{A compartment on a train. MARCELA is looking out the window. She sings.}

Canto del Campo

MARCELA
"Ven aqui, Marcela. Ven a mi,"
the fields wave.
"Ven aqui, Marcela. Ven."
A blush of barley.
"Over here, Marcela. Can you see?"
Fields of corn waving "Come to me."

And I feel the heat upon my skin
As my eyes drink in the brilliant…

CORAL: What are you looking at?

{CORAL is revealed. She is an elderly woman with a youthful countenance. She wears a satin-and-lace dress, and long pearls. Around her neck hangs a small velvet bag.}

MARCELA: Hmm?

CORAL: Out the window?

MARCELA: Corn.

CORAL: Nothing out there.

MARCELA: What do you mean?

CORAL: Twenty-nine August, twenty-nine.

MARCELA: Eh?

CORAL: Nineteen hundred and twenty-nine.
That's when I came here from Santiago.
It was another kind of land then. The fields
gave you a sense of peace.

MARCELA: Did you say Santiago?

CORAL: In Chile. You know it?

MARCELA: No.

CORAL: Right on the Mapocho River, the river
of milk. It can take you straight up to the stars
on a good day.

MARCELA: The stars?

CORAL: "If you ride the river high enough, you can touch the stars, and go straight to Santiago." That's what my father used to say.

MARCELA: Santiago - ?

CORAL: The one in Spain.

MARCELA: The road to Saint James?

CORAL: You've been there?

MARCELA: No. But I've heard…

CORAL: My father dreamed of going there. All his life. He'd say "There is only one Santiago, child. The one in Spain. The rest of us are stars dropped down from the heavens and scattered over the earth. Look up at the sky, child. Look at the Milky Way. You see that star? That's us, that's Santiago *de* Chile. And that one, that shines so brightly it hurts your eyes, that's Santiago in Spain."

MARCELA: Fi-nis-terre. Last place on earth before you reach heaven.

CORAL: You have been there.

MARCELA: No. I've just heard –

CORAL: "Stay close to the river, child," he'd say, "for it is our river that makes the milk of the Milky Way." Of course, that was nineteen hundred and twenty-nine. The Mapocho River's bound to have changed   since last I set eyes on it. Like everything else. Rotten fields…

MARCELA: How can you say that? Look at them. Must be fifteen feet high.

CORAL: Useless.

MARCELA: If there's a Finisterre, it must be here.

CORAL: You think you're close to heaven, child?

MARCELA: I know I'm as far from the ocean as I can get. Nothing but pure earth. All kinds of possibility…

CORAL: I remember when I got here. I was a spit of five. Straight off the boat to New York.

MARCELA: Where buildings are let loose over the sky. … What's it like?

CORAL: The stink of cabbage and fresh fruit. And in the air, a sorrowful blues.

There was a woman named Bessie who walked down my street with a rope of pearls round her neck, and the finest feathers in her hair: *coq rouge*, marabou, and ostrich. She had a voice like thunder. She'd say "My name is Miss Bessie and don't you dare forget it."She was strange. So different from the women in Chile. And she carried herself in such a way as to say "It doesn't matter what anyone thinks of me. I do as I please."

Here I was. A girl of five. Come all the way from Santiago. Didn't know a thing. Could hardly say my name. Coral. Fool name for a child. Cursed name for an old woman.
Can never live up to it. Will always smell death in it. Who wants to know they've been named after a skeleton of small animals?

MARCELA: It's a beautiful name.

CORAL: You think?

MARCELA: It's like the shape of an island in the middle of the sea.

CORAL: It's not "Bessie."
She walked down the street without a care, wrapping her strong laugh around tender young men and tall, wide-hipped women with the smell of marigolds in their hair. I thought,

"I may not know much, but I know what I want. That's the kind of woman I want to be: someone who belongs to everyone and no one, a self-made, self-possessed bird with the taste of poison on her lips."

My father, who'd come with me on the boat to work on Wall Street, would tell me to stay away from Miss Bessie, that she was a "no-good woman, which meant no-good would come of my association with her. But I didn't aspire to any associations, so I could not heed his care-worn advice. Besides, I only saw Miss Bessie once or twice after my father's harsh words.

It wasn't until years later, when I was an awkward thirteen and living scrabble-ass poor in the lower side of the city with some second cousins who had taken me in after my father died that I read in the back of the newspaper, in a column no more than two inches long, that one Bessie Smith had died in a little room in Mississippi, far away from New York and my side of the street, and farther away from my Santiago and all it had meant to me.

MARCELA: It was the singer?

CORAL: The Empress of the Blues. I didn't know a girl like you would know about her.

MARCELA: I know what I've heard.

CORAL: Most of the young I come across think I'm talking about a phantom.

MARCELA: I'd catch her on the radio sometimes, when the signal would come through. Late night station. Would play all sorts: Joplin, Lennon, and Armstrong…
I would press my ear against the radio so I could shut out everything else in the neighborhood and let the songs come into me. At the end of the night, my ear would be burning, and it would hurt to even move my head to one side, but I didn't care, as long as I could go to the places the songs would take me. I remember Bessie because she sang about St. Louie.

CORAL: That she did.

{CORAL sings a line from "St. Louis Blues."}

"St. Louis woman, where's your diamond ring?"

{MARCELA sings another line.}

MARCELA: "I got the St. Louie blues, and that's as blue as I can be."

CORAL: And of course, the first thing I did was go to St. Louis, when I got the chance. I wanted to see the place that she'd named the blues for. I found myself in a whole world of bent rivers. Right smack on the heels of Prohibition's repeal. Now, what is a shy girl of thirteen with a fool name like Coral going to do in a town busting open with liquor and industry, when all she's got is a crooked smile and a couple of dollars slipped into her brassiere?

MARCELA: Whore.

CORAL: That is an unkind word.

MARCELA: I'm sorry. I don't know why –

CORAL: Although it's true. Problem was, I wasn't much good at it. Spent more on soap than what I made in a week. I couldn't stand any other soap but *Maja* from Spain, and they don't just sell that on the street. Not in St. Louis. You got to order that through the catalogue, get it sent down from New York. Pretty soon, I couldn't live on the cheap. Couldn't bathe. Couldn't turn a trick.

I was a no-good woman, half a child, stuck in St. Louis, and damn Spanish to boot. That's what they called me: "The Spanish bit." I kept saying, "I'm from Chile. South America." No one knew what I meant. I thought, "Well, no point me saying anything. Best find me a job somewhere else." I got me machine-work at a brewery. The pay wasn't much better, but it didn't matter if I was clean. As long as I came in at sundown, punched out at sunup, nobody looked at me.

MARCELA: I'd like to go there.

CORAL: To a brewery?

MARCELA: St. Louie.

CORAL: You could go. Town's much changed since I've been there. It's a whole different country now.

{MARCELA looks out the window.}

MARCELA: Miles and miles of rich earth.

CORAL: Miles and miles of waste.

{Pause.}

MARCELA: Where are you off to now?

CORAL: Nowhere.

MARCELA: What do you mean?

CORAL: I ride the trains.

MARCELA: ...You don't - ?

CORAL: No. I don't see much point in setting myself down anywhere. I got no one to tend to, no one to tend me. And that's just fine. That's how it should be. Oh, I was married once. Had a child. The girl doesn't speak to me. Not that I want her to. We have an understanding. I don't come by, no one gets upset.

MARCELA: But you have to -

CORAL: See her? No. She got no use for me. I was a reckless, lovesick mother. Like the song goes.

{CORAL sings from Bessie Smith's "Reckless Blues."}

"And I wasn't nothing but a child.
And I wasn't nothing but a child.
All you men tried to drive me wild..."

MARCELA: ...I used to think that.

CORAL: That you were lovesick?

MARCELA: I didn't think anything of my son. I shouldn't have given birth to him. My mother used to say, back in Santiago –

CORAL: Santiago?

MARCELA: In Cuba. She used to say "You don't want something, you shouldn't bring it into this world." But I thought having a baby would do something, you know, change things. Didn't change anything. Chucho, his father, would have nothing to do with him. And I sure as hell didn't want to be a mother.

CORAL: Like me.

MARCELA: Eh?

CORAL: You loved him, this Chucho?

MARCELA: I thought I did. But he was a shit, you know. He –

CORAL: Couldn't keep his hand in his pocket?

MARCELA: He couldn't keep anything in his pocket. So, I gave him up.

CORAL: Chucho?

MARCELA: My son. I couldn't stand the sight of him.

CORAL: He reminded you of his father?

MARCELA: He reminded me of all men: everything they'd done to me, everything they'd do…The thought of bringing up another in this world… Not by hand. I'd have no part in it. Giving birth was enough.

CORAL: Did you try to kill him?

MARCELA: No. No. Why would you say that?

CORAL: Some mothers do.

MARCELA: I didn't want him, that's all. Not with Chucho gone, and my mother passing…I didn't want a child around. But I think of him. Now. Whenever I see a boy. I think, "What's he like? What does he do? Is his childhood one of ocean, or fire? And does he remember me? Would he remember me?"

CORAL: And what would he think.

MARCELA: Yes. Yes. That too. Which is why I think you should –

CORAL: I don't have that problem. I know exactly what Bessie thinks.

MARCELA: You named your daughter - ?

CORAL: Not that she deserves it. She's not half the bitch Miss Smith was.

MARCELA: ...You can't ride the trains forever. You have to stop sometime.

CORAL: When I'm dead. Oh, don't worry. I'll be dead soon. I've wrestled the moon on plenty an open-mouthed night, and as for the violet-blue chill, I've gotten that too. It's just a matter of time.

{Pause. MARCELA looks out the window.}

MARCELA: Fields upon fields bursting with corn.

CORAL: You'll get sick of it after a while.

MARCELA: What?

CORAL: Bounty.

MARCELA: I can't imagine that I will. Just look at it all shimmering like –

CORAL: You'll start to hunger for stripped skies and leveled smoke, and a place to hang your bloody torso. Cause that's how it will get after a while, after days and days of splitting work: Bloody and broken and filled with crushed charcoal.

MARCELA: In the city maybe.

CORAL: In the country too. You think corn just grows without anybody tending to it,
Without anybody breaking their back over the husks and the leaves and the making of the meal? You'll get so you can't stand the sight of beauty.

You'll start throwing sulfur on the roses, and watch them die. And in the hollow of evening, you will wait for a rumor of grass, so you can un-fence the cancer wrought over this land. Cause it is the suits of the dead you will seek, not the suits of the living. And you will pray for the cancer to spread, and infect everything: The corn, the insects, the trains of milk and syrup, and the sailors, drunk on oil from the rotten sea. And when you read the paper in the morning, you will expect your prayers to have been answered but all you will see is more of everything. Endless bounty.

And you will know that your lovers will remain photographs on a wall, in a breast pocket, in the inside of your seam, and the train will go on past origins and history, and the moon will go unburied. And Christ's children will sail on tiny rafts of twigs burning in the sea, and they will come here, like you, like me, and place their faith in a brilliant fever of a dream because they have spent their lives trembling, their days in want, and it is bounty that they seek, the very bounty that is killing me.

{CORAL begins to cough uncontrollably. MARCELA rises, goes to her.}

MARCELA: Coral? Coral!

CORAL: Get away. Get – away from me!

{CORAL coughs for a bit. A sudden darkness as the train goes through a tunnel, then light.}

You shouldn't stay here.

MARCELA: I've nowhere else.

CORAL: Leave. Get off this train.

MARCELA: I got a ticket. From the kiosk. I got it punched. See?

{MARCELA pulls out a ticket from her pocket, shows it to CORAL. CORAL barely looks at it.}

CORAL: You won't last a week.

MARCELA: You think I haven't been through anything? I've been washing myself out of a bucket for years, walking on dirt roads with bare feet, picking at wounded mangoes to eat. I caught me a stint in prison. Didn't do anything except disturb the peace. I didn't see daylight for a year. Nothing but a hard fixed eternity, and shots of iodine on open skin. And I didn't lie down then. I kept going. Cause I knew there was somewhere else.

CORAL: St. Louie?

MARCELA: I kept this letter.

{MARCELA pulls out folded piece of paper from her bra.}

My Aunt Lise sent it to me. She talks about the greens of this earth, the lush greens, and she's not talking about money. She's talking about possibility, you see? The kind that carries you even if you've got no compass. Like the kind your father talked about when he was talking about Santiago and the stars, about being able to feel connected to something, to feel like your life means something, just by looking up into the sky. And I figure if Aunt Lise found it here…

CORAL: *{to herself}* And the river of milk will take you straight up to the stars.

MARCELA: Eh?

CORAL: How long have you had this letter?

MARCELA: Ever since Lise sent it to me. Must be – oh – twelve years now.

CORAL: And Aunt Lise? Where's she?

MARCELA: Union City.

CORAL: New Jersey?

MARCELA: You've been? What's it like?

CORAL: Can't tell much from the window of a train. …Is that where you're going? This train doesn't go to Jersey.

MARCELA: I took the first train that came by. Saw "St. Louie." I thought it might be close to New Jersey.

CORAL: She's not there, is she?

MARCELA: What do you mean?

CORAL: Lise would've claimed you by now if she was. Everybody who comes here gets claimed somehow.

MARCELA: I didn't ask her to.

CORAL: But you called her, didn't you? You called the number she gave you and someone else answered the phone.

MARCELA: She's bound to show up. She's lived in New Jersey one hell of a long time. Somebody's got to know where she is. Can't everyone have died off.

{CORAL hands MARCELA the letter.}

CORAL: Her handwriting's neat.

(MARCELA slips letter back in her bra. Pause.}

Tell me, you got any money?

MARCELA: For a couple of days.

CORAL: Tell you what, you give it to me now and I won't cause any fuss.

MARCELA: What do you mean?

CORAL: I told you once; I don't want you on this train. You stink of bad luck. You just about gave me a heart attack. I don't need that. I don't need another daughter. I already got one. And I don't tend to her for the very same reason. Cause she makes me upset. She ruins my order. Now, give me your money, and we'll call it even....You want me to start screaming? I'll do it. I'll call the porter and tell him you've been bothering me, that you have been deliberately trying to upset me so you could steal from me – an old woman. You want me to do that?

MARCELA: Is this what you do? You ride the trains all day stealing from people?

CORAL: Come on. Take off your shoes.

MARCELA: How do you know it's -?

CORAL: That's where everybody keeps it when they get here. Come on.

{*CORAL pulls out a small silver gun from her bag, points it at MARCELA.*}

MARCELA: You're crazy.

CORAL: I'll kill you. I've done it before. I don't mind leaving a mess.

MARCELA: {*taking off shoe*} You don't have to do this.

CORAL: No? You live here a while, then tell me what to do.

{*MARCELA takes out a thin wad of bills.*}

What'd you say this would last you? A couple of days?

{*CORAL slips bills into her bag, keeps gun aimed at MARCELA.*}

MARCELA: I told you that was all I had.

CORAL: I believe you.

MARCELA: I just want to ride to the next stop. Then I'll leave. I won't say anything.

CORAL: Why would you? Nobody would believe it. An old tart like me, a half-bit cherry like you. Don't know a damn soul who'd believe it.

{CORAL rises, gun in hand.}

Go on. Look out the window.

MARCELA: ... you'll get caught.

CORAL: How'm I going to get caught if there's no one here? Cause that's what you are no one. Got no one to claim you, come right off the boat, you'll be lucky if you get a proper grave. Go on. Look at the fields of corn.

{CORAL shoots MARCELA once. MARCELA falls. CORAL slips gun back in bag. She sings softly.}

"St. Louis woman. Where's your diamond ring?"

{CORAL walks away. Slight movement from MARCELA. Darkness, as train goes through another tunnel. Music comes up: Perez Prado's "Cerezo Rosa/Cherry Pink and Apple Blossom White."}

Scene four
Hymn to Oblivion

{A slant of sun. A dirt road. MARCELA sings.}

MARCELA
I dream of Cuba.
I dream of snow.
White goose-down over cane and sugar,
White feathers over tobacco and rum.

I am stretched out over the blue and silver
Waves out of which lamentation is spun.
I am stretched out over the curving water
Out of which the iguana wakes at dawn.

All is suspended.
White dogs roam.
The streets cry of gardenias,
And the beating of a tin drum.

In the wake of the morning,
In the ladders of the sun,
I can feel my hips swaying
To the rhythm of an old song:

A wounding *bolero*,
A *guaguanco*,
And a *clave* and *tres*,
Keeping tempo.

A wounding *bolero,*
A *guaguanco*
And a *clave* and *tres,*
Keeping tempo.

Where is the *mamey,*
The coconut and persimmon,
Fruits of my childhood,
Now buried in boats of snow?

I can smell their seeds.
I can taste the delirium
As a thousand sunflowers
Shiver in the cold.

Where is my Cuba?
Where is my son?
My lips turn silver
Looking for your tomb.

*{MARCELA stumbles. Music slowly fades up:
Carlos Nunez' recording of Rosalia de Castro and
Juan Montes' "Black Shadow," as MARCELA
turns to see a WOMAN wearing a dress of silver
rose petals on the edge of the road. WOMEN pulls a
red sash from her dress and hands it to MARCELA.
MARCELA looks at WOMAN, takes the sash, and
begins to tie it around her waist as she rises.
WOMAN smiles and walks away, leaving a trail of
silver petals that shine like newborn stars, in her
wake. MARCELA slowly begins to follow the trail*

of petals. She stops for a moment mid-trail, and looks out. Then she slowly turns, and keeps walking. LIGHTS FADE. Music continues.}

End of Part One

Part Two: In Country

Scene five
Son Viajero

{A metallic light. MARCELA is standing. She
wears the red sash around her waist. She sings.}

MARCELA
The stars fell down from the sky, and said
"You will follow…
silver scraps of gauze on the ground."
As I raised my eyes,
The road spun out
In ribbons, and ribbons of light.

On the corner of *Cinco* and *Jurado*
I saw a man
I saw a man looking at the ground.
He was crouched, he was lost
With his head down.

On the corner of Hudson and Topeka
I saw a cow,
I saw a cow staring at a man.
The same man, but the cow
With her head proud.

On the corner of Avalon and Sunday
I saw a moon,

I saw a moon limping in a door.
The moon wept, it was lost
With her mouth loud.

On the corner of Mission and *Temprano*
I saw a girl,
I saw a girl eating a plum.
She was bent, she laughed
With her head back.

On the corner,
On the corner of Fifteen and Wherever
…I lost my mind.

{Lights fade up to reveal -}

Scene six

{The harbor. MARCELA is standing by the water, humming softly. A sign hangs from an abandoned storefront that reads in Spanish "El Puerto del Vacilon," and under it, in awkward lettering, in English "Port and Ball." RIDER sits under the sign. He wears torn blue jeans, a T-shirt, and a blue sweater, which is at least one size too small for him. His eyes are closed, but he is awake. Occasionally, he twitches. RAFAEL is standing to one side, looking at MARCELA. He wears an old suit, which is a bit too large on him. RAFAEL approaches MARCELA.}

RAFAEL: Need a push?

MARCELA: What?

RAFAEL: Into the water.

MARCELA: No.

RAFAEL: Looks like you want to jump. Like you need a push.

MARCELA: I don't need a push. If I needed one, I would tell you, or I would throw myself in like any other sane person. What I need is to be let be. Ever since I come here, everyone's done nothing but BE at me: Where are you from? Where are you going? Do you want to go by bus or train?… And I think there has got to be a place in this land where where I come from won't determine me, and just when it seems like "maybe…" somebody goes and attacks me for no reason, and robs me of every cent, and shoots me until even I think I'm dead

RAFAEL: You got shot?

MARCELA: {over} until all I got left is to crawl on some train floor, jump off the rail, and walk half awake in country looking for a bit of water, a place to rest. But there is nothing for miles, and my belly starts to ache, and I hitch a bus, train, anything as long as I can move, and stop seeing the road with its signs screaming "Petrol. Cigarettes. German Dutch Apple Pie," cause I am past hungry, and I am starting to feel...

{MARCELA falls onto RAFAEL, passing out. RAFAEL tries to revive her.}

RAFAEL: Hey. Hey. Wake up.

MARCELA: *{barely coming to}* Hmm?

RAFAEL: You got to wake.

{MARCELA passes out again.}

Shit. Hey, Rider. Get me something, will you?

{RIDER opens his eyes.}

RIDER: What?

RAFAEL: *Que esta mujer se me ha desmayado aqui. Traeme algo.*

RIDER: You want some blow?

RAFAEL: No, chico, get me a hamburger, a Coke. She's got to eat. Real food, you know.

RIDER: How bout some fries? Fries are good.

RAFAEL: Just go. Here.

{RAFAEL hands RIDER a twenty-dollar bill.}

RIDER: Twenty?

RAFAEL: Break it for me.

{RIDER stuffs the bill in his pocket, looks at MARCELA.}

RIDER: Hey. She gonna be all right?

RAFAEL: She gets some food she will.

RIDER: You want the corner place or the one over by the station?

RAFAEL: The corner. It's closer, no?

RIDER: Okay.

{RIDER exits. RAFAEL looks at MARCELA.}

RAFAEL: Let's see what we can do here.

{RAFAEL slaps her a bit.}

Hey. *Chica?* Hey. You hear me?

{MARCELA stirs.}

That's right. Awake.

{RAFAEL notices the folded-up letter, which has fallen out of MARCELA's hand, on the ground.}

What's this?

{RAFAEL picks up the letter, smells it, opens it, scans it with his eyes.}

MARCELA: There was this boy.

RAFAEL: Huh?

MARCELA: On the road. He kept staring. With these holes for eyes. I thought he was my son.

RAFAEL: What are you talking about? This is the harbor, not the road. Water. See?

MARCELA: Santiago?

RAFAEL: No. San Diego.

MARCELA: How'd I get - ?

RAFAEL: You passed out. *{indicates letter}* This yours?

MARCELA: My letter, where did you - ?

RAFAEL: It fell.

{RAFAEL hands her the letter. MARCELA slips it back into her bra.}

You'll feel better. I got Rider getting you some stuff.

MARCELA: Rider?

RAFAEL: Hamburger. Something to eat. Tell me. Who's Lise?

MARCELA: My aunt. What's "rider?"

RAFAEL: Rider's a good kid. He works for me. You all right?

MARCELA: Everything's blurry.

RAFAEL: You'll get your eyes back. Come on. Sit up. Straight! There. How's that?

MARCELA: Not so blurry.

RAFAEL: This Lise, your aunt, she lives in Jersey? I had an uncle there once.

MARCELA: You've been?

RAFAEL: No. Too far. He lived in a town called Haledon. You ever heard of it?

MARCELA: No.

RAFAEL: Great town. He was some guy. It's a nice letter your aunt came up with. Lilac paper, huh?

MARCELA: You've got a good nose.

RAFAEL: Don't come across scented paper every day. She must be a nice lady.

MARCELA: I've never met her.

RAFAEL: What'd you mean?

MARCELA: Aunt on my father's side. Just the letter. Phone call once. ...Do I know you?

RAFAEL: I'm Rafael. And you are -?

MARCELA: Marcela.

RAFAEL: Got to get you some food, Marcela.

MARCELA: But I don't got nothing.

RAFAEL: That's all right.

MARCELA: I can't pay for it.

RAFAEL: That's all right.

MARCELA: I'm not sucking your dick.

RAFAEL: Hey. Have I said anything about that? It's just a bit of food we're talking about here. A hamburger, a Coke. What do you want to do? Pass out on everybody? You got to eat, get something in you. And I don't want you to pay me back.

MARCELA: Why not?

RAFAEL: Because I don't. It's just a couple of dollars. Hell. I've been hungry. I know. When I came from *la Republica Dominicana*, I had to live on the street for a while. I had some days I couldn't see straight I was so hungry. I would dirt in my mouth, think I was eating chocolate.

MARCELA: Where in *la Republica?*

RAFAEL: *Santiago de los Caballeros.*

MARCELA: I'm from *Santiago de Cuba.*

RAFAEL: We're neighbors, *como quien dice.*

MARCELA: You've been?

RAFAEL: No. I came from my Santiago straight here. You?

MARCELA: The same. …There was this lady on the train. She said there's a river of milk that goes straight up to the sky and connects all the Santiagos of the earth, all the Santiagos resting on water: Santiago *de Chile, Santiago de los Caballeros, Santiago de Cuba, Santiago de Compostela…*

RAFAEL: That's the kind of crap my uncle in Haledon used to write to me about. Nothing but bullshit. …So, where's your son? You said something about a son before…

MARCELA: No. No. I gave Ambrosio up.

RAFAEL: Ambrosio?

MARCELA: After his father. Everything would call him "Chucho" but his real name was "Ambrosio."

RAFAEL: And the kid is -?

MARCELA: I don't know.

RAFAEL: Same with me. I got a kid down in *la Republica*…Haven't seen him in years.

MARCELA: You miss him?

RAFAEL: I think about him. Sometimes I think I see him. Like you. With that boy on the road.

MARCELA: My whole body aches sometimes just thinking about him. I mean, I gave him to this lady back in Santiago who said she'd take care of him, but… how do you know?

RAFAEL: You don't.

MARCELA: What do you do?

RAFAEL: I don't worry about it. He's there. I'm here. Simple.

MARCELA: I wish I could think like that.

RAFAEL: You're here, aren't you?

{MARCELA moves, almost falls.}

I don't know where the hell this kid Rider – I told him to go to the –

MARCELA: It's just my eyes…

RAFAEL: Sit up. There. …How come you're looking at the water, huh? Fish died a long time ago.

MARCELA: I'm not looking for fish.

RAFAEL: What then?

MARCELA: I missed it. I've seen nothing but land the last couple of days: corn, wheat, sand…I was starting to forget what it was like.

RAFAEL: There's plenty of water here. You cold? It's the Pacific. Pacific Ocean. It's for shit. Nothing but cold water all the time. Cold water, cold air…

MARCELA: You live here.

RAFAEL: Yeah, but I'm not used to it. I still remember *la Republica*, you know.

MARCELA: How long have you been - ?

RAFAEL: Here? Ten years. It's all fucked.

MARCELA: What do you mean?

RAFAEL: Not where I thought I'd be, that's all.

MARCELA: Where'd you think you'd be?

RAFAEL: Nowhere. Nothing. What the hell do I got to tell you for? I don't see you crying. You're hungry, but at least you got someone to get you something.

MARCELA: I didn't ask you to.

RAFAEL: I'm doing it, all right? It's done. …Fucking kid Rider, he's smacked up, you know. Don't make more than fifty a night if I don't watch him.

MARCELA: Fifty?

RAFAEL: He's doing crank, whatnot. Would skip out on the johns if I don't collect for him. Makes me… Fuck. What do I need it for? I've worked the line, made my hundred-and-twenty-five dollars a week cleaning toilets, washing cars. I can do it. But when you got two hundred, three hundred coming in every day, you got to keep going. You can't stop.

MARCELA: That much?

RAFAEL: He don't look it, but Rider's got some ass. The sailors and suits can't get enough of him.

MARCELA: And you?

RAFAEL: I do him every once in a while. Got to make sure he's still sharp. I keep Rider out of trouble. He'd be dead by now if I wasn't around.

MARCELA: But the money's good, isn't it? You're like everybody else…

RAFAEL: Listen, when I came here, I thought all sorts of things. I thought "Hell. I'll make myself a million."So I took the straight path, right? Straight and true. Didn't get me anywhere. No matter how much I missed Linda and her red beans a rice. And her *mojito* was great. No question about it. But Linda wasn't paying, you see? Linda was down in my Santiago getting by: looking at the stars, praying to God, and asking me to send her cans of condensed milk and pounds of sugar. So I took a different path, cause I wasn't about to get by. A drop of fag's blood, a drop of sailor's blood, what's the difference? It's blood. We all swim in it.

MARCELA: And Rider?

RAFAEL: Rider does his dead-eye-dick routine and goes home.

MARCELA: And where's that?

RAFAEL: Here by the port, down by the station. Wherever he can, you know.

{RIDER enters with a white paper bag in hand.}

Hey. Rider.

RIDER: Hey. *{To MARCELA}* You're awake.

MARCELA: Yes.

RIDER: You look good.

RAFAEL: What you got?

RIDER: Huh?

RAFAEL: In the bag.

RIDER: They only had fries.

RAFAEL: No hamburger?

RIDER: I didn't see it.

{RIDER hands MARCELA one bag of fries from inside the paper bag, keeps another bag of fries for himself.}

{*To MARCELA*} You were splayed like a starfish.

MARCELA: What?

RIDER: Before. When you were passed out. Legs and arms all... I thought "What kind of glass jellyfish I got to break to dive into your muff?"

RAFAEL: Rider!

RIDER: What?

RAFAEL: Enough! {*To MARCELA*} I'm sorry. He's not used to talking to people.

RIDER: What'd I say?

RAFAEL: Nothing. Just shut up. {*To MARCELA*} Hey. Eat them slow, all right? You don't want to shock your stomach.

RIDER: {*To RAFAEL*} She don't like sea stuff?

RAFAEL: Not now, all right?

RIDER: I like the sea. I like getting lost. {*He eats from his bag of fries*}

RAFAEL: {*indicating her fries*} So, they're good?

MARCELA: They're fine.

RIDER: Sometimes I get up in the morning, and stare at the sea for hours.

RAFAEL: *{To MARCELA}* You've had them before?

MARCELA: Not like this.

RIDER: And I count all the dead fish that have washed ashore.

RAFAEL: *{To RAFAEL}* They were thicker, huh? Real potatoes. Not like this shit they got here.

MARCELA: They're fine. Really. A little crunchy, but –

RIDER: There was this walleye once…

RAFAEL: Back in my Santiago they cut up the potatoes and serve them to you fried in big chunky slices like it's supposed to be. Right from the earth, you know.

RIDER: …spooked me.

RAFAEL: And then they drop them down on your plate, and… you can't mistake it for anything but a potato. Here? You don't even know what you're eating. Where'd you get this shit, eh? Rider? Where'd you get this shit?

RIDER: At the station.

RAFAEL: I thought I told you to go to the corner place.

RIDER: It was busy.

RAFAEL: At this hour?

RIDER: The line was all the way around. Folks were stepping over each other for fries.

RAFAEL: What else did you get?

RIDER: Huh?

RAFAEL: I gave you a twenty. Where's the change?

RIDER: …Fuck. They didn't give it to me.

RAFAEL: You're going to tell me you stood there with a twenty, bought two extra large bags of fries, and nobody gave you anything?

RIDER: They gave me the fries.

RAFAEL: Empty your pockets.

MARCELA: Maybe they didn't give it to him.

RAFAEL: You eat your fries and shut up. *{To RIDER}* Empty.

RIDER: But I'm still eating.

{RAFAEL grabs RIDER's bag of fries out of his hands, and squashes them under foot.}

RAFAEL: There. You finished eating.

RIDER: I don't got it.

RAFAEL: Well, you didn't just split. I know you. You plaster those sad eyes on that damn cashier until he has to give you coin, even if you're not supposed to get it. So, where is it? Or was there something else you got at the station?

{RAFAEL cuffs RIDER.}

RIDER: Hey. You're going to screw up my diges-

RAFAEL: It's already screwed. What else did you get?

MARCELA: He already told you what happened. There's no need to hit him for it.

RAFAEL: Where'd you come from? Nobody ever gets hit in your Santiago?

MARCELA: All the time. But there's no need for it.

RIDER: She's got something there, Raf.

RAFAEL: …You like this kid, don't you? You want him? You can buy him right now. I'll sell him to you for thirty bucks.

RIDER: Hey. Wait a minute.

RAFAEL: You're right. Twenty-five. Bargain price. He don't need much. Just a pet every so often. Look at those eyes, those cherry lips. And he's got a ripe ass. You like his ass? He'll even fuck you. He don't just do boys.

RIDER: I'm best meat.

RAFAEL: You got twenty-five? Do you? You should buy him now. He won't be much use for long. They want them fresh these days.

RIDER: I'm fresh.

MARCELA: I don't think…

RIDER: I'm plenty use. I can get anyone anytime.

RAFAEL: What are you talking about?

RIDER: Why'd you say that, huh? Fucking make me look…

RAFAEL: Hey. You want this sweet girl to buy you? Give a smile. Teeth. Come on. …

MARCELA: Why – why are you doing this?

RAFAEL: Cause you like him. I want to do good by you. After all, you've come all the way from Cuba. Land of the *jineteras.*

RIDER: Like rum and shit?

MARCELA: I am not a *jinetera.*

RAFAEL: You've never screwed for dollars?

MARCELA: Not everybody in Cuba is a whore.

RAFAEL: I tell you what; I'll give him to you for twenty. Same as what the fries cost.

RIDER: Hey. I thought you were going for twenty-five.

RAFAEL: Twenty. Bottom price. You got it, Marcela?

MARCELA: ...No.

RAFAEL: What's that?

MARCELA: No, *cabron de mierda carajo.*

RIDER: I bet if we had gone for twenty-five...

RAFAEL: She don't got it, Rider.

MARCELA: I'm sorry.

RIDER: You're flat out? That's no good. You always got to keep something on you. Hey. You like pinball?

MARCELA: What?

RIDER: They got this old machine down by the station. It's a mean game.

RAFAEL: Rider! I thought I told you to do something.

RIDER: What?

MARCELA: Don't hit him again. Please.

RAFAEL: You really like this kid, don't you? He must look a bit like your son. What was his name again?

MARCELA: Ambrosio.

RAFAEL: Ambrosio. That's right. I bet a kid like yours would go for prime dollars in the right market.

MARCELA: Don't you tell me anything, *hijo de puta cabron*. Not a goddamn –

{RAFAEL hits MARCELA.}

RIDER: She ain't done nothing, Raf. She's just broke.

RAFAEL: You. Empty your pockets. *{To MARCELA}* You listening to me? Is this what you want?

MARCELA: I can't think…

RAFAEL: Come on. Eat your fries.

MARCELA: I can't.

RAFAEL: I won't have you getting sick on me. Come on now. Put the fries in your mouth.

{RAFAEL hits her again.}

Eat.

{MARCELA slowly begins to eat again as RAFAEL watches.}

And no tears. I won't have my girl crying. I paid twenty dollars for those fries.

{RIDER has emptied his pockets. Some gum wrappers, candy wrappers, rubbers, book of matches, vending machine trinkets on the ground.}

RIDER: Hey. Raf! Over here… See?

RAFAEL: Put that shit back in your pockets.

RIDER: I told you I didn't have anything.

{RIDER puts items back in pockets.}

RAFAEL: Yeah? So, what's that?

RIDER: What?

RAFAEL: Up your nose?

{*RAFAEL cuffs him again.*}

RIDER: What the fuck -?

RAFAEL: Where's the change, Rider?

MARCELA: Let him be. Can't you do that?

RAFAEL: You got twenty? You get twenty; you can bite his ripe ass.

MARCELA: You're just like Chucho. He'd damn sell anything to get by.

RAFAEL: Hey. This kid here is like a son, you understand? I'd do anything for him.

MARCELA: Yeah, but when the shit falls –

RAFAEL: When the shit comes down, I don't let anybody hide under a table.

RIDER: Look, there was this guy, all right?

RAFAEL: {*To MARCELA*} What did I tell you?

RIDER: He had on this hat. Real sharp.

MARCELA: …Nothing but scratch and tear at anything for a lousy buck….

RAFAEL: You're going to eat or you're going to talk?

MARCELA: Eat shit.

{RAFAEL grabs bag of fries from MARCELA and walks toward the water. Is about to dump fries…}

No. Don't. Please. Rafael! I'll eat them.

RAFAEL: What?

MARCELA: Please.

(RAFAEL throws bag of fries to the ground in front of MARCELA. MARCELA goes about gathering the fries and eating them off the ground.)

RAFAEL: He was a sharp guy, eh?

RIDER: You want me to help you pick those up?

MARCELA: I got it.

RAFAEL: So, the guy…

RIDER: Yeah. Yeah. I went up to him.

RAFAEL: With your fries?

RIDER: This was before the fries.

RAFAEL: Before the fries?

RIDER: Yeah. This was as I was coming into the station.

RAFAEL: So you had no intention of going to the corner place.

RIDER: He was real sharp this guy. You should've seen him. He had on this designer top and a watch: some kind of foreign number I ain't ever seen with gold swirls and shit. And he had his hair slicked back like one of those rich sods that bag off in the islands… Fuck. My nose is hurting. I got to rest up.

RAFAEL: Later.

RIDER: But it's hurting now.

MARCELA: Let him rest. His nose is all busted.

RIDER: I must look like shit.

RAFAEL: You're beautiful. You know that.

RIDER: Best meat?

RAFAEL: Best meat. Now tell me about the guy. You went up to him and -?

RIDER: Yeah. Yeah. I asked him for a cigarette. Casual, right? I don't want to start something and have him turn on me; you know what I'm saying? He says he don't smoke, but would I buy him the paper over by the stand. He looks at me like a real ass bandit. I'm thinking "He don't just want the paper. He wants a fancy rubber or some kind of cock giz." So I go to the stand.

RAFAEL: And you buy the paper.

RIDER: Wall Street J. And one of those smell-o-rama rubbers. "Pine Dream" or something. Fucking car wash kind of name.

RAFAEL: And that's what? Five dollars?

MARCELA: My head hurts.

RIDER: You want me to get you something?

MARCELA: I can't breathe.

RIDER: I got some reds might do you –

{RAFAEL cuffs RIDER.}

What do you got to hit me for, huh? Can't you just tell me stuff? Sailors don't like bruises, man.

RAFAEL: Suits do. And they pay, right?

RIDER: Right. Right. So, like, nothing, he takes the Wall Street J.

MARCELA: I need water…

{MARCELA goes toward the water.}

RIDER: And he puts it under his arm. And not a "thank you," right? Like he's used to being served. I look at him, and put my hand where he can see it. Casual. I don't want to play him rough, cause he's sharp, this guy.

{MARCELA does not vomit, but remains doubled over for a bit. During the following she will slowly straighten up.}

So I turns towards track fifteen. You know.

RAFAEL: Figuring he'll follow you down.

RIDER: Yeah. But he doesn't. He gets real cold. Blue ice. I figure I spooked him, whatnot, that's the end of that.

RAFAEL: But you didn't leave. You figured he was spooked, but you stayed with him.

RIDER: He put his arm on me. Real tight. His eyes were one big, wet stare. I thought "All right. Let's give this colt a ride." But he says he's got something else in mind. I say "I don't do nothing without green up-front." He starts squeezing my arm. And he won't let go. He is staring. Like he knows something deep, right? I'm thinking "Damn. If he don't want to fuck, what does this creep-ass want?" So I get real gentle, and start to lick his arm, the one he's got on me, letting my tongue go down right down on his sunburn. His grip starts to get less hard. He starts to smile a bit. And I say "I am your blue horse rider, your sea-horse diver, and if you keep smiling, I'll take you anywhere you want."

RAFAEL: I like that.

RIDER: That's pretty good, huh? Worked a charm.

{MARCELA starts to walk away.}

Hey. You okay?

RAFAEL: She just had to put her head down a bit. Breathe in the salt water, right?

{RAFAEL goes to touch her.}

MARCELA: Don't. Don't! …I haven't finished eating my fries.

{MARCELA resumes eating last remaining fries slowly.}

RAFAEL: *{To RIDER}* So, you're licking.

RIDER: Yeah. But I can't wait for him to drop change on me all day, so I say "Give me fifty now and I'll do you right here in the terminal." He drops his arm. Quick. And he says, "Give me all you got." I think, "This guy's lying, right?" But I see he is serious cause he starts looking at the cops like he's going to rat on me if don't do WHAT, so I give it to him.

RAFAEL: What?

RIDER: Ten-er. That was all I had.

RAFAEL: And the other five?

RIDER: Got the fries. I had to keep something in my back pocket.

RAFAEL: Liar. Piss-ante liar.

RIDER: It's the truth.

RAFAEL: You met that guy. Right. And you balled him straight up and he paid you.

RIDER: No. It wasn't like that.

RAFAEL: And you took his fifty and my twenty, and you went over to track fifteen, and you got yourself some blow.

RIDER: No.

RAFAEL: And when you finished putting it up your nose, you said to yourself "Fuck. I'm hungry." So you went over to the Pup Stop, and got two bags of fries, which comes to two dollars in change, which is all you had today, or don't you think I check your pockets in the morning? You must think I'm one slow card not to check your pockets.

RIDER: The Pup Stop was closed.

RAFAEL: Not only did you take my twenty, given to you in good faith, but you went round and made yourself a fifty without even thinking about keeping a thirty for my take. And then you come to me with this piss-ante story, this goddamn tale from the winds, and you think I'm going to take it? You are one lying bent-fuck son-of-a-bitch.

{RAFAEL pulls a switchblade from his suit pocket.}

MARCELA: What are you -?

RAFAEL: Stay out of this.

RIDER: Not my face. Anything. But not my face.

RAFAEL: Your face? Doll, I wouldn't dream of touching your face. How else am I going to get my seventy back, huh?

{RAFAEL starts to cut RIDER with the switchblade.}

Seventy. And eighty-five percent more from here after. You get me?

{RAFAEL continues to cut RIDER.}

Meat!

{RIDER staggers.}

MARCELA: Stop.

{*RAFAEL continues.*}

RAFAEL: Maggot!

MARCELA: Stop.

RAFAEL: Lying bitch!

MARCELA: STOP. STOP. STOP IT.

{*RIDER collapses. RAFAEL approaches fallen RIDER and carefully wipes the switchblade clean with an un-bloodied part of RIDER's clothes. Then steps away from RIDER and puts switchblade back in suit.*}

Goddamn son-of-a-bitch.

RAFAEL: Shh. It's all right. Come on now.

MARCELA: Get off me. Fucking bastard.

RAFAEL: …All right. All right. Come on, Rider. Let's clean you up. Let's go.

{*RIDER stirs.*}

RIDER: The sea…

RAFAEL: That's right. Back to work.

RIDER: I got – headache.

RAFAEL: We'll fix you right up.

RIDER: …fuck.

{RAFAEL pulls RIDER up. RIDER can barely stand.}

RAFAEL: The suits are going to love you like this, Rider. They'll love you.

RIDER: Yeah?

{RAFAEL kisses RIDER lightly. RIDER smiles, tries to walk. MARCELA looks at RAFAEL.}

RAFAEL: What are you looking at?

MARCELA: …Nothing.

RIDER: Raf? Raf?!

RAFAEL: I'm here, Rider. I'm right here.

{RAFAEL puts one of RIDER's arms around him, and drags him along, as they exit. MARCELA *remains. Slight pause. She puts her hand to her chest, clutches the letter.}*

Scene seven

{The harbor. Between darkness and light. MARCELA is huddled near the water. She is shivering.}

MARCELA: "There are sunflowers that touch the sky, and..." Where, Lise? Tell me.

{From off, MIRIAM MOCHA is heard singing Bessie Smith's "Reckless Blues."}

MOCHA: "And I wasn't nothing but a child..."

MARCELA: *{To herself}* Coral...?

{MIRIAM MOCHA enters on a makeshift wheelchair. She wears a cotton eyelet top and dark pants, over which is draped a thin blanket onto which are pinned small handwritten scraps of paper. Her hair is short.}

MOCHA: *{continues song}* "All you men tried to drive me wild..."

MARCELA: Give me a dollar. Dollar. Give it to me.

MOCHA
MOCHA: I'm looking for coin myself to take me across the border.

MARCELA: Everybody's looking for coin. See the yolk of that pale star? It's turned to piss.

MOCHA: What happened to you?

MARCELA: Everybody wants something. Sometimes even when you're not after anything, things come after you.
I come here to rest, after getting stuck on some train bound I-don't-even-know-where, and I end up here by the water, blue and cold. And I'm not looking for anything, but there's always some Joe, cept in this case his name is Rafael, and I didn't know, how was I to know ?

MOCHA: He struck you?

MARCELA: Up one side of the face, down the other. So there's your answer. Neat. Cept I don't think it is. The way I see it, there's nothing neat. If there was, I wouldn't be here, I'd be in New Jersey living my aunt in her red-brick house, making a real go of it, you know, instead of in this place, this damn furnace of the spirit, where I can't even cast myself against the fury of heaven cause everything's so rotten. What the hell is this place anyway?

MOCHA: This is the West. Land of Billy, Jesse, and all the other outlaws they got in the history books. Didn't you get no schooling?

MARCELA: Not that kind.

MOCHA: I got mine real early. My old man sat me down when we were in –

MARCELA: Santiago?

MOCHA: Santiago del Estero. How'd you know?

MARCELA: A guess.

MOCHA: Some guess. I don't even got an accent, cept when I talk damn fast. Then everything goes to crap.

MARCELA: And this Santiago is in - ?

MOCHA: Argentina. Everything's kind of forgotten down there on account of it being at the southernmost tip of the world. It's the last place on earth, really.

MARCELA: Last place on earth before you reach heaven?

MOCHA: More like the last place on earth before you reach hell. Argentina's pretty far south. I lived there til I was twelve. Right on the *Rio Dulce*, the sweet river. It was so sweet it was said that it must have been the saints who christened it upon setting their tongues on it.

MARCELA: How come you were reading history books about the West in Argentina?

MOCHA: How come folks read about China in Finland? Everybody everywhere wants to be somewhere else. My father wanted me to come here. He'd say "mocha," that's what he called me, even though I'd been named Miriam by my mother.

MARCELA: Mocha?

MOCHA: Cause of my short hair. He'd say "you have to know everything about everything if you're to go out West." He said if the North as a whole was damn peculiar, then the West was even more so. And he was right. It isn't just the biggest goddamn snakes you see here, but God-amazing white field roses that look like they have been dropped down from Canaan or some other forgotten place. And desert blue nights where you swear you can see five moons lit up in the sky all at once like a freak sign of nature.

MARCELA: Five moons?

MOCHA: As if all the Santiagos in the world were connected to this band of sky.

MARCELA: The Milky Way.

MOCHA: More like the ghost of Saint James himself, who instead of choosing in which Santiago to rest his soul, has let himself be scattered among the five moons, and so shine down on this spot of earth, in hope that some pilgrim will take this as a sign of comfort along her travels, and be relieved from the weariness of the road.

MARCELA: In the dark sky, when I was on the water on the boat of scrap lumber on my way from Cuba to here, I saw five moons lit up at different points in the sky, and I thought of my Santiago.

MOCHA: Saint James. A piece of him on each moon, on each star. His body stretched out from one part of America to the other.

MARCELA: And I thought "If I just stay close to the sky, I'll find my way."

MOCHA: Land and sky connected to each other all because of a name, all because of a restless saint. And in the morning, after the five moons have lit up, the sky turns black, for an instant.

MARCELA: The sky turned black before the plane…

MOCHA: Then slowly you see grains of light come down from heaven bloody amber, and you're not sure what they are: whether they are the tears of Saint James, or just shards of clouds broken up by the sun's rays. All you know is for a moment your whole being is swept away in that delirious sky. That's the peculiar thing about the West. You never know if what you're seeing is real or made up.…That's why my father thought if there was anywhere I could make something of myself without fear of being disappeared, it'd be here in this peculiar place, but I ain't made much. Sure as hell not like the outlaws did.

MARCELA: I could still go.

MOCHA: What'd you mean?

MARCELA: To New Jersey.

MOCHA: You ever been to Jersey? It's as rough as this place is peculiar.

MARCELA: You've been?

MOCHA: *{Indicates handwritten notes pinned onto her blanket}* See all this? This is everywhere I've been.

MARCELA: *{looking at notes}* Kansas, Chicago, Wyoming...

MOCHA: I got tired of remembering, so I started to write every place down. There 's no mistaking where I'm at this way.

MARCELA: *{finding note on blanket}* New Jersey.

MOCHA: Yeah. Spent a couple of days there out by an old amusement park.

MARCELA: What was it like?

MOCHA: Kind of gray, brick houses, blind cats running around. The ferris wheel was broke. I don't see much reason why you'd want to go there, when you can cut across the border with me.

MARCELA: I got to go to New Jersey. I got to know if my aunt's there.

MOCHA: Why?

MARCELA: She's my last living relative, except for my son.

MOCHA: You've a child?

MARCELA: Ambrosio. He's in Santiago somewhere.

MOCHA: Santiago -?

MARCELA: In Cuba.

MOCHA: You've got no one else?

MARCELA: Everyone else in my family has died off. … I have this letter…

{MARCELA pulls out the letter from her bra.}

I've had it so long I don't know what to believe anymore.

MOCHA: Let me see.

{MARCELA hands letter to MOCHA. MOCHA opens it, reads.}

MARCELA: I used to be able to make out about half of what she said. But now that I'm here…I got to know what's become of her, one way or the other, even if it's only for my own mind, not knowing makes me feel like there's a piece of me missing, floating out in sky somewhere.

{MOCHA closes letter, hands letter back to MARCELA.}

MOCHA: You should get yourself fixed up, if you're to go anywhere. Nobody will take you in looking like that.

MARCELA: Who said I wanted taking in?

MOCHA: You got to look presentable, not all bruised and… you should get some good shoes, and fix your hair. Here. I got a ribbon you can use.

{MOCHA pulls a ribbon from under her blanket.}

Piece of satin I picked up. It will dress you up right quick. You don't want it?

MARCELA: It's yours.

MOCHA: I can get another. People throw stuff out here all the time. Come here. Let me put it on you. I got a knack for fixing people right.

{MARCELA draws near to MOCHA. MOCHA starts combing MARCELA's hair with her fingers.}

MARCELA: This what you do?

MOCHA: Ambulatory hair salon. That's right. I do a bit of everything. Your hair is a right mess. When's the last time you combed this thing?

MARCELA: Before I got on the boat. When I got off the boat. Don't know after that…

MOCHA: If I had a real comb, I'd do you right.

MARCELA: I don't even know what I look like anymore.

MOCHA: You got to get yourself a mirror. I had one, but it got broke by some asshole that had nothing better to do than smash up what didn't belong to him.

{MOCHA finishes combing through MARCELA's hair.}

How that feel?

MARCELA: Better.

MOCHA: Looks better. Now for the ribbon.

MARCELA: Don't pull it too tight.

MOCHA: I know what I'm doing.

{MOCHA ties ribbon into MARCELA's hair.}

There. Damn near great.

MARCELA: Yeah?

MOCHA: Better than it was.

MARCELA: I wish I had a mirror. I can't remember the last time I had a look at myself.

MOCHA: *{pointing to abandoned storefront}* You could look in that broke-up pane there. I often catch myself in it sometimes.

{MARCELA goes to storefront, looks at herself in window.}

MOCHA: What?

MARCELA: I can't see anything.

MOCHA: Look in the water. It's pretty clear this time of day.

MARCELA: The water. Yes.

{MARCELA goes to the water, looks.}

…I don't recognize myself. My skin is hollow, lips broken, and my eyes…

MOCHA: You're tired. That's all.

MARCELA: I've been assassinated by the sky. Marcela has died,
 Drowned in the ocean's well,
Covered in seaweed and stagnant black water.

And it is I who have been left,
This I without a name, without a country –
This spectral I who roams the land
Escaping from wounds newly bled,
With a cold spoon in her open mouth,
And a serpent at her throat.

This I who is Christ's child and Judas' child,
And the child of a trembling earth,
Who awakens in the dark
Tormented by kisses,
And the scratch of a phantom baby at her belly,
And a sky who rains blisters on the streets,
Who seeks tribute from those who beat her…

And in the mean time, in the mean time,
Oh, the ghost of Marcela cries
like a fresh sea-wind
Flaring in the broken waves
so its spirit can bleed.
And this I looks at the ghost of Marcela
And says "Wherefore," and "How has it been,"
While all the while begging for solace
 on mercury's rim.

Oh to be christened now with another name,
A name that will fit this sun-patched,
stone-bruised I
Who is eternally homesick?
As befits one from this land
Where homesickness is a national disease.
Christen me, Mocha. In the here and now,
christen me.

MOCHA: What'd you mean?

MARCELA: Give me a name.

MOCHA: I ain't about to baptize you.

MARCELA: Christen me, or I will take yours.

MOCHA: …Sharon

MARCELA: Sha-ron. Sharon, Sharon, Sharon. It tastes funny in my mouth, but if I keep saying it…Sharon, Sharon…

MOCHA: I didn't know know putting a ribbon on you would make you crazy.

MARCELA: Perhaps this is what being on newfound earth, and seeing yourself for real, does to a person.

MOCHA: You need a real mirror is what you need. Not some ocean full of dead fish. Come on, we'll get on a bus, and go across the border. We'll go all the way back to Santiago –

MARCELA: No. I'm going to New Jersey.

MOCHA: I thought "Marcela" had died.

MARCELA: …One last thing.

{MARCELA kisses MOCHA's hand, then starts to walk away.}

MOCHA: Hey. How are you going to get there without any coin?

MARCELA: I'll find a way.

{MARCELA walks away.}

MOCHA: Watch yourself now. Don't go walking around all crazy just cause you got that ribbon in your hair.

{MARCELA smiles, exits. Pause. MOCHA softly hums a bar from Bessie Smith's "St.Louis Blues," and exits.}

Scene eight
Canto Uno: The Sell

{The train platform. MARCELA sings in Spanish.}

MARCELA
Santiago.
Te busco en los escombros,
En los altos y los bajos,
En la sangre del anhelo
De tu grito redentor.

Santiago.
Te busco en los brazos,
En lo lejos y lo extrano,
En los rotos y vacios
De tu alma seductora

Santiago.
En el fondo de tus mares,
En tus noches y tu cana,
En tus senos y entranas

Dame besos de calor.

Dame brisa
Dame arena
Dame gotas
De tu boca negra.
Dame aire y viento
Y esquinas sin furor.

Santiago.

{MAN* appears in half-light.}

Mi alma se esta muriendo
Sin tus suenos,
Sin tu amor.

Canto Dos, Variation: The Transaction

{On the train. MARCELA is on her back. HALf-DRESSED MAN* is on top of her. This is visually abstracted. She sings:}

MARCELA
Santiago,
I look for you in the arms
In the far-off and the strange,
In the rupture and the hollows of your
seductive soul.

Santiago

From the bottom of your oceans,
From your nights, your cane,
Give me your fevered kisses.

Give me breeze
Give me sand
Give me milk
From your dark mouth.
Give me the air, and wind
From your unrelenting tongue.

Santiago
My soul is dying
Without your dreams
Without your love.

*{The HALF-DRESSED MAN dismounts her,
adjusts his pants. He pulls a handful of dollars from
his pants pocket, and throws them at MARCELA's
feet. He exits. MARCELA picks up the dollars.}*

Scene nine

*{Behind an empty kiosk off a road. MARCELA is
leaning against the kiosk. PACO is fondling her.}*

MARCELA: Tall grass and columbine.

PACO: *Que?*

MARCELA: I can see it from here.

PACO: Is that where you are from? Tall grass and - ?

MARCELA: Yes. That's where I'm from.

PACO: There was a girl in my village. She looked a little like you. We called her "Perla. Perlita." You sure you've never been to Cuba?

MARCELA: I'm from here.

PACO: Sharon?

MARCELA: Right.

PACO: How is it, then, you smell of jasmine?

MARCELA: Stop.

PACO: You do. You smell of jasmine and the sea. I looked at you and said "This is my Perlita from the ocean. My Perla *de oro.*"

MARCELA: My name's Sharon.

PACO: Yes. But inside. You're my Perlita, aren't you?

MARCELA: Don't.

PACO: Just a kiss. What's wrong?

MARCELA: Empty your pockets. Come on, Paco.

PACO: *Que?*

{MARCELA draws a knife from inside her sash.}

MARCELA: Give me all you got.

{MARCELA cuts him.}

PACO: *Co~no*.

MARCELA: Take off your shoes. Come on.

PACO: How do you know it's in my -?

MARCELA: That's where everybody keeps it when they get here.

PACO: You're crazy.

MARCELA: I'll cut you whole.

PACO: I only got a couple dollars.

MARCELA: I'll take it.

{PACO begins to take out folded-up bills from his shoes.}

MARCELA: *{counting bills}* Thirty, forty… What's that? Around your neck?

PACO: It's a coin. My nana gave me it. I wore it round my neck when I was on the boat. For protection. See? It's got a *concha* on it.

MARCELA: A *concha?*

PACO: The sign of Saint James.

MARCELA: Give it.

PACO: It's not worth anything.

{She cuts him again.}

Co~no carajo…

MARCELA: You won't need it.

{PACO hands her necklace.}

PACO: You're crazy. Everybody's crazy here.

MARCELA: Go on now. Go!

PACO: I don't even know where I am.

MARCELA: You'll find your way.

PACO: …Crazy.

{PACO walks away. MARCELA drops the knife, tucks dollars inside bra, holds onto the coin for a moment, and then tosses it to the ground. She doubles over, as if to vomit. Silver coins begin to tumble out of her mouth as music comes up: Bessie Smith's "Do Your Duty." MARCELA looks at the silver coins, not knowing quite what to do with them. After a moment, she gathers them and puts them in her pocket. She looks out. Music continues.}

Scene ten

{A harsh sun. An abandoned lot covered with snow. MARCELA is looking at the lot. She wears a new dress, shoes, and a wide-brimmed summer hat. The red sash remains around her waist. CARLO is standing to one side. He wears a long coat, sweater, pants, and nondescript shoes.}

CARLO: You can't stand out here all day. You'll catch cold.

MARCELA: I just want to look at it.

CARLO: You've never seen snow?

MARCELA: No.

CARLO: Doesn't last too long, the effect of it. Oh, it's beautiful. But once you start seeing it every day, you don't think of it as anything except a nuisance, something you have to shovel, fall into for a certain number of days. And then it goes, and you let it go like rain. And that's when you start to think of it like you're looking at it now: as something wholly of this earth yet altogether strange.

MARCELA: And beautiful.

CARLO: And beautiful. Yes.

MARCELA: ...Can't believe it got torn down.

CARLO: What?

MARCELA: Lise's house.

{CARLO takes off his coat.}

CARLO: Here. Put this on.

{He goes to drape coat over MARCELA's shoulders.}

MARCELA: Don't touch me, all right! I don't want you touching me. Not here. Not now.

CARLO: …Put it on yourself. I got no problem with that. …Go on.

MARCELA: Yeah?

{CARLO nods. He offers her coat. MARCELA puts it on.}

CARLO: I just don't want you catching your death out here, have people blame me for it.

MARCELA: Why would they blame you?

CARLO: Cause I'm standing here talking to you. Simple as that. And you're standing there with that damn hat.

MARCELA: I saw the sun out my window, out the train, and I thought it must be hot, "let me get a hat." I didn't know the sun could be out, and it could be cold. I've never known that to be so before.

CARLO: What'd you say your name was again?

MARCELA: Sharon.

CARLO: Funny kind of name for someone from Cuba.

MARCELA: It's my given name. Lise knew me by another.

CARLO: What was that?

MARCELA: Marcela.

CARLO: I like that.

MARCELA: It's a common name.

CARLO: So's Sharon.

MARCELA: But it suits me. It suits me better than my own. I don't know Marcela anymore. But I know Sharon. I pass by a window; I can spot her in a second with or without a hat.

CARLO: My folks changed their name when they came here. This was way back, before I was born. They wanted to sound like they belonged, so they went from Pietroponte to Cahill in one day. But when it came time to name me, they went ahead and called me Carlo after my dead uncle. I've spent my whole life stuck with the ill-sounding name of Carlo Cahill just because my folks wanted to belong.

MARCELA: Doesn't sound too bad.

CARLO: Sounds godawful when you put it next to other people's names. But I can't change it. Not now. I've lived with it too long. But you've got a perfectly good name, one you were born with. It may not sound right, here, now, but I bet it'll come to suit you fine.

{He draws near to her.}

MARCELA: You must think I'm some kind of Cuban trash.

CARLO: I don't think that.

MARCELA: That I'm only good for dirt jobs and fucking, that I'm not good enough to be called Sharon or any other name except whore, and worm, and wetback, even though I got about as much right as anybody to seek out what I came for. You've done nothing but look me up and down like I just came out of water and ash, like some kind of prodigal who's come here to steal snow from your lots –

CARLO: I never said –

MARCELA: You want to throw me money, like you're doing me a big favor? I got money. I got goddamn silver coins nobody wants. I got hard cash that can take me clear up to the mountains, if that's what I want. But I'm here, right? I'm here cause I thought I could find somebody, somebody who'd tell me about the purple sunflowers that rise up in the twilight and tear the clouds wide open, and the dazzling brightness of stars that burn your eyes, but everything is a lie. There's nothing sacred, nothing noble. There are no angels hidden in anybody's cheek. There are only rocks on water, sharp razors, and the pain of gunpowder in my eyes. And you tell me I'm not good enough? I think I am more than good to carry anybody's name around here.

CARLO: You're fine.

MARCELA: You bet I am.

{She starts to walk away.}

CARLO: I'm sorry your aunt couldn't see you.

MARCELA: You knew Lise?

CARLO: She always went to the market where I work nights. She always bought the same things: black beans in a can, white rice, and cocktail franks. Sometimes she'd throw in a bottle of wine, sweet old wine from Spain that we kept stashed in a corner.

MARCELA: From Malaga?

CARLO: What?

MARCELA: The wine.

CARLO: It was from Spain. That's all I know. Lise liked it. I'd tease her "Hey Lise, you got a hot date tonight?"Just being a kid, you know. And she'd smile, and gather her paper bag and wave at me. "Sure I do," she'd say, moving her hips lightly as she walked away. ...Sometimes I'd see her at church. She had these big heavy black rosary beads she'd carry. Make a hell of a racket. And she always wore a red sash around her waist, like the one you got. Made the priests real nervous. Would scare off the congregation. But she wore it anyway. She said she had to keep the spirits of the earth in line, keep protected, and red was the only color strong enough to do it. Any other color would put the earth off balance. I couldn't figure her out, but I didn't mind. It was Lise, you know. It was all right. ...Then I stopped seeing her. At the market, at church. Wasn't long it seemed before I heard she'd died. And then some time later, the house got torn down. Nothing but brick-stacks and a couple of stray cats running around. And I... I forgot about her.

MARCELA: She sent me this letter.

{MARCELA pulls letter out of her bra, hands it to CARLO.}

Doesn't seem like that long ago.

CARLO: This is from Lise?

{MARCELA nods. CARLO opens letter scans it with his eyes. After a moment, he closes the letter.}

CARLO: It's been some time.

{CARLO hands letter back to her. MARCELA begins to tear the letter to pieces.}

Hey. What are you -? Stop that.

MARCELA: Last bit of Cuba I got left to get rid of, last bit of fucking… I can't walk around with a dead woman's letter next to my skin. Will start to feel dead myself.

{MARCELA finishes tearing up the letter, tosses the pieces into the air. Pause.}

CARLO: What now?

MARCELA: I don't know.

CARLO: You can't stay out here.

MARCELA: No, although it sure feels good to look at snow. Ambrosio might like it here.

CARLO: Who?

MARCELA: This little boy I know....You must be freezing without your coat.

{MARCELA starts to slip off coat, CARLO stops her.}

CARLO: I'm all right. The sun actually does warm things up a bit.

MARCELA: *{Simultaneous}* You want -?

CARLO: *{Simultaneous}* You want -?

MARCELA: Go ahead.

CARLO: I was just going to say… if you wanted a drink or –

MARCELA: No.

CARLO: Oh.

MARCELA: Not yet.

CARLO: But later?

MARCELA: Maybe.

CARLO: …So, I'm at the market til eleven or so. The one on Lincoln. It's got a red sign and banners. You can't miss it. And if you do, you just turn round the corner, and we're right there. Cause we're a whole block. A square, you know? So…

{CARLO starts to walk away.}

MARCELA: Your coat.

CARLO: Oh, that's all right. Keep it. You'll need it for the cold.

MARCELA: Thanks.

{CARLO walks away, then stops.}

CARLO: Marcela?

MARCELA: *Que?*

CARLO: Nothing. Nothing at all.

{CARLO exits. Beat. MARCELA slowly unties the red sash around her waist. As she does so, the faint sound of the sea. MARCELA lays out the sash

carefully on the snow. SOUND and LIGHTS
FADE.}

Scene eleven
Memento: The Letter

{A band of blue and green laid out flatly against the
sky. MARCELA is standing. She speaks from
memory.}

MARCELA
"Querida Marcela,
In my heart I do not have the words to tell you
what I feel, what I think about this land.
I write to you on this paper
 that smells of lilac to tell you
that if you want to come here, you can stay in
my home. I have nothing else to offer.
Ask of me nothing else.

The trees are bare, and there is a bitter
nightfall.
And sometimes I hear voices at midnight that
speak of murder. But if you want it, it is yours.
The sky's delirium may protect you,
And the copper clouds
may find a way into your heart,
As they have not found a way
completely into mine.
Perhaps if you think of the equator, and its
invisible line, you will find constancy here.

There is a blond liquor-seller on the main
street, shouting
 like those you used to hear in Cuba.
He speaks a strange tongue but he reminds me
of days you probably do not even remember.
There is an abandoned church at the end of
another street, where I sometimes go when I
want to be truly alone,
where the only sound you can hear
is the one of the subterranean traffic with its
incessant rumble and odd hum…"

I eat green figs in the winter from the corner
market, which seems to never run of stock.
And I smoke cigarettes at any time I please,
sampling a different brand each week without
ever being able to smoke the same brand twice.

Sometimes I swear I can see the lights of
Santiago shining in this mad sky,
And hear the voice of Saint James himself
whisper to me in the clear of night.
But often it is just copper and gray,
And there is only the liquid trace
of a star's path
to remind me from where I came.

It is a labyrinth here
Of smoke-stained windows,
of purple-brown air,

and hints of blue and green.
I often lose track of time,
and space seems ever more elastic.
But I remember everything,
everything I see –
Santiago,
The black water
The bridge at the edge of the sea –
There is so much to hold in one's memory
That Cuba fades now to silverpoint

Something like this.

{MARCELA looks out. Slight shift of light. She begins to sing a variation on the Invocation from Part One.}

Santiago (Coda)

The palm of Santiago
Burns in the sky,
As another Santiago
Shines in the night.

And a pale arm of Santiagos
All around me.
A rain of silver light
That longs to guide me.

On this ground of concrete,
On this ashen floor,

The stars of Santiago
Let my heart be restored.

*{The band of blue and green against the sky
dissolves into a field of stars.}*

END OF PLAY

PERDITA GRACIA

Synopsis:

In a town in the Florida Keys, a young woman named Perdita seeks new love, while she is haunted by the memory of her mother. A magical story of a couple, a marriage and abandoned selves staking out new territory.

Characters:

PERDITA, impulsive, intelligent, and prone to dreaming

HERMIONE, Perdita's mother (live and mediated), a guide, a ghost, a soap-opera vision: long-suffering, and filled with forgiveness

FLORI, Perdita's fiancé, brash, attractive, ambitious, and a bit confused

BOSCO, Perdita's guardian, a fisherman, adventurous with a seemingly unlikely Romantic spirit

FRIP, Bosco's friend, wise, put-upon, generous and a bit of a fool.

AXL, a rogue*, an outlaw, an apparition, part of this time and another

TIME, a surfer punk

LEON, Hermione's husband (mediated)*, calculating, stubborn, unyielding

RAVENS, a chorus of androgynous angels. runaway kids

Place: An island, an ice floe, and a pool of light.

Note: * The role of Axl may be played by a woman. The role of Leon may be doubled with Frip. Melodies to the original songs in text may be obtained by contacting the author.

Script History

This piece was originally commissioned and presented by Denison University Department of Theatre, Granville, Ohio as part of a Jonathan R. Reynolds Playwriting Residency. It was subsequently presented at New York Stage and Film/Powerhouse Theater in an outdoor production directed by Debbie Saivetz. Further development of the piece was sustained at New Dramatists and Ripe Time Company in New York City.

Poor thing, condemned to loss"

Antigonus

<u>The Winter's Tale</u>, Act II, 3

Part One

1.

[Perdita is seen in a slant of light.]

PERDITA
It's like this: I was born. Like any other child.
Into the world.
Into a great big world too big to dream about.
With nothing on me
but new flesh and the imprint of my father,
a father I did not even know, cause he didn't
want anything to do with me.
He didn't even want to see me.
This is what I'm told. This is what I've heard.
This is my rumor and gossip:

My mother was in disgrace, because of his
jealousy.
She was exiled and abandoned, left with only
me inside her.
She cried. I felt her tears inside the womb.
Her tears flowed into me and gave me breath.
And I swam in that breath,
and I dreamed of her:
I dreamed inside her because that is what
children do before they're born:
They dream without thinking.

[Hermione, Perdita's mother, is heard singing a section from "A losing child" from Off.]

HERMIONE: No daughter of mine...
No, no daughter
Will see this world...

PERDITA: Her voice had such goodness I wanted to taste it.

[Hermione continues singing...]

HERMIONE: Poor child, Poor child...

PERDITA: I wanted to put her voice in my mouth and have it fill me.
I wanted so much I was born before my time.
Out. Pop. Whoa. I was eager.
But eagerness didn't do much for me.
I didn't even see my mother
before I was taken from her.

I was wrapped up
and tossed from one hand to the next.
"What are we to do with her?"
"What are we to do?"
"Cast her to the fire," said one. Then another
suggested "Dash her brains out."
Then another said
"Leave her to the kites and ravens."

[The chorus of Ravens is seen.]

There was a savage storm and I was left on
shore, left to the elements.
This is what I've heard, this is what I'm told,
this is my story:
A man found me.
He took pity on the poor lost thing before him
and named me Perdita: one who is lost.
It serves me well, for I am lost to myself. That
is my destiny.

2.

[By the sea.]

FLORI: Give me a match.

PERDITA: What for?

FLORI: Cigarette.

PERDITA: You need some wine.

FLORI: Says who?

PERDITA: I do.

FLORI: You're weird.

PERDITA: I'm who I am.

FLORI: How come I like being with you?

PERDITA: I don't know. Maybe you've lost your mind.

FLORI: Perdita.

PERDITA: Shh..

FLORI: What? No one's going to -

PERDITA: My father might.

FLORI: He's not even your father.

PERDITA: He raised me. He's what I know.

FLORI: He won't care.

PERDITA: He's got a temper. You don't know him.

FLORI: Bosco? I know him plenty. He does errands for my step-dad all the time. Bosco's a damn good fisherman.

PERDITA: It's in his blood.

FLORI: But he's still good at it. Some people inherit a talent or a skill and they're crap, no matter how hard they try.

PERDITA: What'd you inherit?

FLORI : I don't know.

PERDITA: Aren't you good at anything?

FLORI: I'm good with numbers. I can add things up, figure things out.

PERDITA: Is that all?

FLORI: I'm good with you.

PERDITA: What's that mean?

FLORI: Hanging out, being with you, talking and stuff.

PERDITA: That's not something you've inherited.

FLORI: No, but I'm still good at it.

PERDITA: You are so full of yourself. You think you've got me wrapped, don't you?

FLORI: I don't think anything. I'm just here.
We're just hanging.

PERDITA: Just, just, just, yeah. You must think
I'm stupid.

FLORI: I don't think anything.

PERDITA: …That's why I love you.

FLORI: Do you?

PERDITA: That's what I'm good at.

FLORI: Stop.

PERDITA: Aren't I? Willful, up to no matter,
reckless girl, stopping too long to talk,
to look, to let herself be looked… just think the
stories that have been told about me.

FLORI: There are no stories.

PERDITA: That's cause you don't listen.

FLORI: To who?

PERDITA: Sky angels, ravens…

FLORI: The eyeliner kids who squat outside
the church, the runaway freaks? They just say

things to say them. That's what they do. They make noise.

PERDITA: You should listen.

FLORI: Why should I listen to them when I can be here with you?

PERDITA: You're nothing but compliments, Flori.

FLORI: Say it again. My name. Say it.

PERDITA: Flori.

FLORI: I love how you say it.

PERDITA: What else have you been smoking?

FLORI: I love you. I love you, Perdita.

PERDITA: We said we wouldn't complicate things.

FLORI: Who's complicating anything?

PERDITA: Love. That's a complicated word, Flori.

FLORI: It is not. It's the simplest word in the world. I love you. How simple is that?

PERDITA: I just want to have a cig, ok? Can I do that, Flori?

FLORI: You treat me like a girl.

PERDITA: Well, you do have a girl's name.

FLORI: It's Florindo, I told you. Except I don't like it, that's all, so I go by Flori.

PERDITA: Flower girl. My sweet, delicate Flori.

FLORI: I'm not.

PERDITA: What? You're not sweet?

FLORI: I'm not delicate.

PERDITA: Show me.

FLORI: No.

PERDITA: Why not?

FLORI: Because it's not my nature to show. When the time comes, I will do.

PERDITA: You have a lot of rules for yourself.

FLORI: A person has to live by things.

PERDITA: I don't live by anything.

FLORI: You're completely free?

PERDITA: I live by nature, its rules, its chaos, its misery, its science and beauty. I give myself over to the earth and the sea, cause they're what made me. What else should I live by? People are always trying to figure themselves out, making up rules and predicting how they'll change, and defining themselves and others against some standard they think has been set in stone somewhere. We burden ourselves until we turn into closed-off creatures living by impossible rules that have nothing to do with nature and its order and randomness, and then we wonder "why can't we figure ourselves out?" Well, we could if we spent more time just living, you know.

FLORI: Like getting married? Don't you want to?

PERDITA: Oh, Flori, you're too funny.

FLORI: I have feelings, you know.

PERDITA: I know, Flori, but why make such a fuss? We're having a good time. Let's have it.

FLORI: I want a fuss. I want someone to damn fuss over me. I'm tired of this hanging around, let's-see-what-we-do shit. I want something real, you know, something I can name, hold onto. I mean, what are we? We're always hanging out, sharing stuff, telling each other way too much, all sorts of deep things we wouldn't tell anybody, or just hanging cause we do, cause we get along, and that's great, don't get me wrong, but it only goes so far, you know, before you want something else, something a little more, okay, old-fashioned right? Like what your grandparents had or if you're lucky, your parents had...or someone you met once said they had. That's you want. That's what I want. I want a goddamn fuss. Don't you love me?

PERDITA: I just don't think we should be so serious.

FLORI: You love someone else? Who is it? Frank? Mitchell? Sebastian? It's him, isn't it? I've seen you looking at him.

PERDITA: I don't....

FLORI: You walk into the market and make eyes at him, and flirt like a schoolgirl. Like he's going to give you anything. He's got a cold heart and a cold mind. And you're all goo-goo about him, aren't you?

PERDITA: I'm not goo-goo about Sebastian.

FLORI: Then who? One of the ravens? You're in love with one of the eyeliner kids, one of the runaway freaks? Which one? The one with the full lips? He's always looking at you. He's always staring.

PERDITA: I don't love anyone else.

FLORI: You're always thinking about somebody else. Always looking to see who's out there, when I'm goddamn right in front of you, patient and loyal as a damn dog. That's what you think of me, isn't it? I'm your dog. I'm your play fellow. I'm your damn sport.

PERDITA: Look at that pelican. You think it's thinking about who loves him or not? He's just perched on that rock letting the sun on him, taking the warmth in. We should give that pelican credit for knowing a thing or two. We should enjoy the sun. Get some wine. Just be, you know. That's the hardest thing to do and nobody realizes it.

FLORI: You're going to make me crazy, Perdita.

PERDITA: You already are.

FLORI: I'm not.

PERDITA: Loving me? Yeah. You are. And that's a good thing.

[Shift. Ravens appear. They are androgynous angels with digital eyes.]

RAVEN 2: Be true to him, brat.

PERDITA: Don't call me that.

RAVEN 1: Brat you are cause we have named you. Be true.

PERDITA: I am true.

RAVEN 1: No eyes for any other, brat?

RAVEN 3: No eyes for me?

PERDITA: …Eyes are made to look. I choose what I see.

[Perdita walks away with Flori.]

RAVEN 1: Smart one, isn't she?

RAVEN 3: She's got a mouth.

RAVEN 1: She's quick.

RAVEN 3: Transparent girl.

RAVEN 2: Is she?

RAVEN 3: Transparent to the quick. Loves more than she admits.

RAVEN 1: Brat. Loves more than she should.

RAVEN 2: Doesn't know anything else.

RAVEN 1: Lost one. Brat.

RAVEN 2: Brat.

RAVEN 3: Bastard girl. She wants me.

3.

[Night. Along the harborwalk. Revelers.]

BOSCO: If I knew where I was going, I'd be a hell of a lot farther along than I am now.

FRIP: You're doing fine, Bosco.

BOSCO: I do what I can. But there's no money in fishing anymore. Everybody wants things out of a can. Processed, ready-to-go. A real live fish scares people. Cause they forget, you know. They forget that what they eat comes from the earth and not from some antiseptic place.

FRIP: You're making sense, Bosco.

BOSCO: For a drunk man, I suppose I am.

FRIP: You're not drunk.

BOSCO: No, you are, Frip.

FRIP: We both are, truth be told. Where's Perdita?

BOSCO: I haven't seen her.

FRIP: What'd you mean?

BOSCO: She's been seeing a lot of that Flori boy. She's my one joy in life, and if she chooses wrong, what am I to do?

FRIP: Counsel her.

BOSCO: Hard to counsel anyone when it comes to love. Love seeks its own counsel.

That's the truth of it. You try to untangle a love, you'll end up in a heap somewhere, on the dirt, and always thought of as a meddler. I would hate for someone to think of me thus. But I still lie in bed at night and worry and there's nothing that will make me wake fresh as morning mint.

FRIP: Trust her. That's what you have to do.

BOSCO: You're not her father. Easy for you to say.

FRIP: Trust is all you have.

BOSCO: I see how Flori looks at her. He's deep in love.

FRIP: And she's not?

BOSCO: She's distracted.

FRIP: That's a sure sign. Love drives one to distraction.

BOSCO: To ecstasy, eh?

FRIP: That's the ancient word for it. I prefer "distraction."

BOSCO: Wish I were distracted.

FRIP: You're past love, Bosco. It's come and gone for you.

BOSCO: And how do you know that? I could meet the love of my life tomorrow.

FRIP: In a blink, eh?

BOSCO: I'm still an attractive man.

FRIP: I don't think you're an opsimath.

BOSCO: What the hell's that? Is that one of your damn words?

FRIP: It's another old one. Means one who finds things late in life. That's not you, Bosco. You already found your things.

BOSCO: What? A child? Found her. Yes. But I didn't choose her. Not the same. Not love like you read about or see in the flickers. Not love that turns you round and under and messes up your brain. You see? That's what I want. Something that makes me crazy, that turns me round, so I don't know where I am, so I can find something else about me.

FRIP: That's philosophy.

BOSCO: It's not. It's real life. I've seen it happen. I'm telling you, I could still have that.

FRIP: Maybe you'll find a mermaid.

BOSCO: Mermaids are a myth. Death's what they are. They lead sailors to their death.

FRIP: That's one story of many. You can't go believing everything you hear.

BOSCO: A non-mythical creature is what I want: a living woman, not a death wish.

FRIP: The mermaid I've seen is plenty woman.

BOSCO: Where'd you see her?

FRIP: When we were on the boat a couple of weeks ago. She rose up and gave me a look. She had dewy skin, and hazel eyes.

BOSCO: You were close enough to see her eyes?

FRIP: They were very hazel. And she had long arms. Very elegant.

BOSCO: Hazel eyes? I love hazel eyes. And I love the sea. We're perfect for each other.

FRIP: Now you believe in mermaids?

BOSCO: You've seen her. It's good enough for me.

FRIP: What about Flori? Aren't you going to talk to him?

BOSCO: About what?

FRIP: He's getting serious with Perdita, isn't he?

BOSCO: They've got all the time in the world. What's the rush? If I had that kind of time... What a damn clear night it is.

FRIP: Nothing but stars out.

BOSCO: I wish I knew their names. I didn't get far in school. I didn't like studying. My father was a fisherman, and my grandfather, too. It was clear enough I'd follow suit. But I didn't know things would change, that it would be harder and harder to make a living at sea.

[Axl appears. He is beat up.]

AXL: A better living than I have made.

FRIP: What happened to you, stranger?

AXL: I was robbed, that's what. Every dime on me gone. And I used to be quite the man in my time. Had riches all about me.

FRIP: You're a sight. Did you get beat?

AXL: They roughed me up, yeah. Kicks and mitts. Steel toes they had right in my skin. Damn loose ones loosing about, twisting the shiv, thinking themselves lit matches struck by some divine right to make a mess. Left me powerless, and broke as all get...

FRIP: Kilkenny cats, eh?

AXL: What's that?

FRIP: Relentless bastards who fight to the end.

AXL: If that's the word you use for them, yeah. They were the very thing. Kilkenny. A contrary band, they were, a band of hellkites contributing to the disruption of all order. I got pains in my calves and stomach, not to mention queasy about the head. My head's gone swimmy. That's a fact. That's a clear sputter. My skull's full of squalor. Is that ale you got? I'm thirsty as can be. To run through country without a drop, and then get attacked by some hellkites is enough to do any man in.

BOSCO: Did you get a look at them?

AXL: Nah. It was pitch dark. They came up behind me. Kicked me right away. I was down on the ground before I knew anything. I wanted to catch sight but one of them gave me a look fit to smithereen glass.

FRIP: Hellkites all around these days. Kilkenny cats and hellkites.

AXL: They took every bit from me. They knew their business.

FRIP: They're smart. You can't let yourself wander.

AXL: I didn't. I was looking for a job. Just got fired. I thought I'd take another route, try my luck.

FRIP: And look what you found.

BOSCO: It's a cruel world.

AXL: And I'm at its mercy.

FRIP: Have you lost all your money truly? ...Don't feel right knowing that. *[takes wallet out of his pocket]*. I could offer you some, stranger.

AXL: I couldn't take your kindness. I'd be in your debt. And I don't have the means to be in anyone's debt. Not just yet.

FRIP: But who was it that robbed you? Did you catch a name?

AXL: Only name I heard was Axl. He must have been the leader.

FRIP: I had a cousin who got beat up by him. Took every cent he had right down the pisser.

AXL: This ale is rich. Where'd you get it?

BOSCO: The Green Parrot. They hide this ale in the back.

AXL: When I get some money on me, I'll buy you a tankful of ale just for being kind and offering a worn man something to drink.

BOSCO: No thanks needed. You need it more than I. I'm past drinking. We've been drinking all night, haven't we, Frip?

FRIP: Once you start…

BOSCO: Exactly. At day's end, a pint or two

FRIP: Or three

BOSCO: Puts your mind at rest.

AXL: And what have you got to worry about?

FRIP: He's got a daughter.

BOSCO: I've plenty worries for her well being in this world.

AXL: My old man was always worrying about me. Even when he split on me, I knew he was worrying.

BOSCO: A father's duty is always incomplete.

FRIP: There now, Bosco, you're going to start crying.

BOSCO: Am I getting weepy, Frip?

FRIP: Your eyes are brimming.

BOSCO: Blasted ale, blasted fish, blasted water that gives too little to a man, I'm to bed.

FRIP: You want me to wait up for Perdita?

BOSCO: She'll be around in time. She's always looking for her mother.

AXL: What?

BOSCO: She thinks she'll see her if she looks hard enough. There are worse things in the world than chasing after a dream.

[Bosco and Frip walk away.]

AXL: Thanks for the ale.

FRIP: Ale's for nothing, for a long night. If you need anything, don't be afraid to ask, stranger.

AXL: I'll pay you in kind.

FRIP: One man does for another. That's enough.

[Bosco exits, followed by Frip.]

AXL: And so I sit on dock's edge, free ale in my hand and more to come, if I play my cards right. Axl's my name. I am the very hellkite. Bit of story I told back there to those two. It's best to be incognito, see what the game is, before you play anything. These bruises? They're nothing. They're powder. And my clothes have been torn for a long time. It's all a game. When you lose a job, you got to find another. An outlaw only lives in the public imagination for so long before he's forgotten. You have to keep making yourself new all the time, just to keep going. So, I've taken to stealing. And it's kept me for a while. All I can say is whatever I've done, heaven's been on my side.

[He sings:]

"Pale moon"

And the pale moon shines at night
Weary as a ragged bitch
I wander and let hell be my guide
Fingers got the mighty itch.
Come on, come on, fingers
Save me from redemption, from redemption...
Do the all-mighty trick.

[Axl reveals he has stolen Frip's wallet.]

4.

[Lone road.]

FLORI: Can't see anything on this road. Nothing but trees. What's so special about this place anyway?

PERDITA: You'll see.

FLORI: If I didn't love you…

PERDITA: She'll appear if we're really quiet.

FLORI: Who?

PERDITA: My mother. Don't you want to see her?

FLORI: You don't even know who your mom is.

PERDITA: She looks just like me.

FLORI: Perdita, it's late. We should get back.

PERDITA: Don't you want a midnight kiss? A midnight kiss in the middle of an empty road with the ruins of a monastery down the way. A clear night and nothing but us. Can you think of anything better?

FLORI: You tempt me.

PERDITA: I'm a raven, a spider, I'll catch you.

FLORI: Stop. Perdita…

PERDITA: …There's a light.

[A glow, as if on a screen….]

Can you see it? Can you see her?

[The image of Hermione is seen, suspended in space.]

FLORI: She looks just like you. Is she your mom?

PERDITA: I believe she is.

FLORI: Where's she coming from?

PERDITA: From the sky.

HERMIONE: What are you saying?

FLORI: She's talking to me.

PERDITA: She's not.

HERMIONE: Speak to me.

FLORI: I'm Flori. I'm the man who's in love with your daughter.

HERMIONE: Why do you wound me?

FLORI: What's she talking about?

PERDITA: She's not talking to you.

HERMIONE: Why do you cause such suffering
in my heart? You have never known me to be
anything but true, and now you accuse me
Each night I get up and wonder when you will
come back to bed, when you will surrender
your pride and let go of the lunacy that is
inside you. Each night I wait for your caress
and there is nothing because you have lost
faith in me. I have only been true, my love.
That is my weakness.

FLORI: She's crying. Her tears flow into me.
They give me breath. I think I'm dreaming of
her, Perdita, the way you do.

PERDITA: We're both dreaming.

FLORI: I feel ashamed, Perdita, and I don't
even know why.

HERMIONE: All the goodness has been
drained from you. You wish to punish some
part of yourself and instead you punish me.

FLORI: Who has hurt you so? Tell me.

[*Image fades.*]

Where is she?

PERDITA: I don't know. She always disappears in the same place.

FLORI: Bring her back.

PERDITA: I can't.

FLORI: You conjured her, didn't you? Bring her back.

PERDITA: I didn't do anything. She appears like this every night. The same story, the same words, and then it stops, and it's over.

FLORI: Do you think that is what love does to people?

PERDITA: I think love does what it does. It has its own path. It asks for the impossible in a person because that is the only thing worth doing.

FLORI: I just know I don't want to ever be like that: jealous and mean and hurtful to someone, to make someone suffer like that. I don't want to live with remorse in my heart, Perdita. It's ruin, absolute ruin.

PERDITA: You believe that?

FLORI: Yes.

[She kisses him.]

Why'd you do that?

PERDITA: Midnight kiss. I promised you, didn't I? I'm true to my word.

[Perdita and Flori fade into each other. Time shift. Ravens appear.]

RAVEN 2: Divine shape he

RAVEN 1: All night out by the monastery

RAVEN 2: They found themselves

ALL RAVENS: Wrapped

RAVEN 2: Until dawn break

RAVEN 1: Until tide swept

RAVEN 3: Until the crash of a motorbike on I-70.

RAVEN 1: I saw them.

RAVEN 2: I saw them.

RAVEN 3: Brat and her intended to be.

RAVEN 1: Nature's playthings.

RAVEN 3: But she still has eyes for me.

RAVEN 1: In your dreams.

RAVEN 3: In dreams that we live, yeah, in dreaming eyes that yield to me.

5.

[Inside the house. Perdita sleeps.]

BOSCO: You know what I fear, don't you? That I will lose you, that's what. I think about it all the time. You don't know because you're young but when you've lived a bit, you think about dying and what it means and how it can happen just like that, like on the water, at high sea. Every moment is counted. I used to go out in my boat and just think of the fish and what had to be done for the day. I was alert to the sky and its patterns and the movement of the ocean, but nothing else. It was just me and the boat. And now I'm out there on the water and I forget the time, but everything gets clearer and clearer – the ocean, the sky, the trees on the islands…The bluegills are moving through the water and the sun is falling in lucid slants. And I see this creature, right? With angled eyes and no shame, pre-God-like, a pagan thing, and this creature is damn smiling at me, and I think "this is a dream, let me toy with it," cause dreams are nothing but toys we give ourselves or someone gives to us. And so I say "Hallo." And this creature with angled eyes speaks back to me in a strange liquid tongue, and for a moment I think I'm some other where – on a glacier with a lone plane circling the sky above me…And this creature says to me "What are you waiting for?" Just like that in plain English. And I think "I don't know. What am I waiting for?"

All my life has been about you. From the day I found you I've had no thought to anything except how to raise you, how to change nappies right, and be a mom and dad for you. And I've been a good father, even if I'm not really yours. But well, now I have raised you, and what? You'll leave me. Cause that's what children do. So you have to understand, Perdita, it's my time now, right? You have your beloved. Flori's a good man. But well, I've got to fill my heart. Before I lose all time.

[Bosco kisses her gently, and walks away. Perdita wakes.]

PERDITA: Father?

[Bosco exits.]

6.

[In the square.]

FRIP: Have you seen Bosco?

AXL: Not a glimpse.

FRIP: He comes by every afternoon and now he's disappeared on me. Is that right?

AXL: I wouldn't know.

FRIP: Where'd you say you were from again?

AXL: Up north. Where the world sits in wait for all manner of catastrophe.

[Frip exits.]

7.

[A boat on the water.]

PERDITA: Do you see him?

FLORI: I don't see anything.

PERDITA: …How long has it been?

FLORI: I've lost track of time.

PERDITA: …We should go back. …I'm scared, Flori. We should've seen his boat by now.

FLORI: …What's that?

PERDITA: What?

FLORI: A bit further out.

PERDITA: I can't tell anymore.

FLORI: It's a person. Or an animal. I don't know.

PERDITA: I'm cold. There's no sign, Flori. Father's gone. Truly gone.

FLORI: I think I can catch it.

PERDITA: What are you chasing?

FLORI: A pair of eyes.

PERDITA: You're seeing things.

FLORI: The moon on the water. I can see everything. I'm not afraid, Perdita. I'm not afraid of anything.

PERDITA: …Tell me you love me.

FLORI: I love you.

PERDITA: …Tell me how we'll be.

FLORI: Caring and tender until we grow old, until all we have is a dream of our youth, a dream about ourselves now on this water, under the moon's stare, looking for your father, looking for something gone, looking because it is all we can do, because it is what we have sworn to each other, because we are children, and all children can do is look up and out and hope and pray and not curse the sky when it rains. We are children and one day we will be parents, and when we are, our children will look up to us and seek and not cease in their seeking because they will think we have answers we have never had. And our youth will overwhelm us because it is the best part of ourselves, of our memory, of our love. And I will see you in your dress, in your wedding dress made of silk and lacy light, and I will hold you night after night without tiring ever of your flesh, of your sweetness, and of the things I don't understand, because there is nothing left to understand when all is clear. Here on the water I see eyes gazing at me. They ask me to move forward, to keep searching, to keep true to my promise. And I do.

8.

[Flori is asleep on the boat. Perdita is awake. The moon is dying. Raven 3 appears.]

RAVEN 3: Dream me.

PERDITA: …Your hands are smooth, marble cold.

RAVEN 3: Your legs extend. Wrap me.

PERDITA: Strange feathers and clear eyes. Feathers that caress my back and tickle my neck. I'd like to be a bird.

RAVEN 3: You want to fly?

PERDITA: I want to be small, hide in trees. I want to be very small and be able to see everything (like you).

RAVEN 3: Like your mother?

PERDITA: Like everyone I miss. Inside I miss things, things I don't know, can't imagine. I'm rumor's child trying to retrieve memory when all I remember is my mother's cry.

RAVEN 3: You are a sad one.

PERDITA: And you are a beautiful bird.

RAVEN 3: I'm harsh. My feathers are sharp. They cut.

PERDITA: You are made of air. Air and water.

RAVEN 3: In the sky on water and sand I am yours like a remnant thing, a remnant of history, half forgotten, half remembered…

PERDITA: You make yourself up.

RAVEN 3: Your tears flow into me.
And I will follow.

PERDITA: I give you breath.

RAVEN 3: And I will follow.

PERDITA: Our breath is one.

RAVEN 3: And I will follow.

PERDITA: Because this is what home is like.

RAVEN 3: Be home to me. Give me things. Fill me up.

PERDITA: Make me.

[The moon dies.]

9.

[Day. On the water. Flori is awake. Perdita is stirring.]

FLORI: No sign. I thought I saw something, but…

PERDITA: Mirage.

FLORI: Is that what it was?

PERDITA: It's what happens at sea.

FLORI: We're almost home again.

PERDITA: I can't even remember father. His face is fading from me.

FLORI: You need to sleep.

PERDITA: When is our wedding, Flori?

FLORI: Soon.

PERDITA: Days and days?

FLORI: Sooner than we think.

PERDITA: I wish it was tomorrow. I wish it was right now.

FLORI: My sweet Perdita… are you all right?

PERDITA: You're so good to me, Flori. You've been so good to look for father.

FLORI: We're almost home.

PERDITA: I dream so much. Why is that, Flori?

FLORI: Because dreams bring peace.

PERDITA: Do they?

FLORI: Either that, or more dreams.

[Perdita sings]

"Nothing lost"

PERDITA: Dream in the darkest hour
Dream while the light is green
Dream in the silent hour
Dream while the light is green
Nothing made of nothing lost
Nothing made of this.
Nothing made of nothing lost.
Don't slip away from me.
Don't run away from me.

[A raven flies overhead.]

End of Part One

Part Two

10.

[Ten years later.]

FRIP: Lost, lost, lost rotten, and more lost,
everyone leaves, it's a shattered marketplace,
No fish on sale, no one wants anything, they
want pre-cut, frozen, plastic slices for their
Crate & Barrel plates to go with their
Abercrombie & Fitch clothes. It's a sad and
miserable waste of a waste of lostness vast and
trapped on this island. I told him, I told him,
"stay on, friend. Don't leave, Bosco." But he
left, not to return, and the stranger has
not been seen since either. Ten years of waiting
and lostness and losing sense. And now it's
cold, too. No one to talk to. Everyone gone. I sit
by the ocean and watch the fish drown in the
oil slick.

[Time appears as a surfer punk.]

TIME: I ride waves to keep myself going.
I scope out the mutants
and play hopscotch with people's brains.
I retrieve gestures and send messages.
And sometimes I just stop
Whoa, okay, no time for this.

I'm time's face. I take everything in.

Speeded up in stitches, wrecking order,
holding hope in my hands,
I try my luck in the modern age and ask myself
"Is this it? Like this alone, together?
When did this start? Last night?
A quarter of a century ago?
At twilight time, aching time, breathing time,
and hey, sister, I-need-some-wine ago?"
Or was there something pivotal
 that turned ten years into a different age:
a reflecting pool of extreme desires,
skeevy impulses and moving trucks?
I'm time's face. My radar is on the go.

[He sings:]

"Come buy"

Come buy of me; come buy, come buy.
Buy, boys, or your girls will cry.
Come buy. Come buy.

[spoken] I am steady on
dropping nothing cause what else is there to
do but go on and keep going?
I stand watch over the acid revelers
and the ecstatic suits
and the arcade junkies fresh out of quarters

and the WWF acolytes waiting with steely
gazes for the next match:
throw-down and blood seen.
I stand watch over the soccer thugs with their
rude ready smirks and glazed ale eyes,
and countless women on the rush, on the go,
making good the economy;
women mourning and carrying on life's lot,
TIME IMMEMORIAL,
while new fathers
are buried in asphalt and fire.
I'm time's face. I take everything in.

I see everything with my sunglasses on
I've got the ultraviolet held back for centuries.
And I cry
 and do not let my tears fall ten years past
cause they don't stand a chance
against the tick-tock of the human.
I don't even know about clocks.
 I didn't invent them.
They were created to measure days in bits,
 and suffocate freedom.
I'm before clocks. I'm part of eternity.
I'm time's face. I take everything in.

I'm now, past and after.
I'm the constant lover and faithful friend,
and I am always taken for granted.
Under the rock, under the mat, hell's
apprentice and heaven's messenger.

I'm nothing but what you live and dream.
Inscribe a place for me in your memory.

*[Time disappears round a sky corner and catches
another wave, as Raven 1 and 2 appear, clubbed-out
angels a bit past their prime.]*

RAVEN 2: This place is so…

RAVEN 1: This place is shiny rotten screwed
up.

RAVEN 2: Crapped out and messed up.

RAVEN 1: Fake plastic tangled yeah.

RAVEN 2: How long have we been in this nitid
place?

RAVEN 1: I don't remember anymore. I don't
remember anything.

RAVEN 2: We can't even stand in front of the
church cause nobody gives. Everybody's
holding onto their pocket.

RAVEN 1: Yeah, they think if they hold on,
they won't lose anything. When everything's
lost.

[Raven 3 appears]

RAVEN 3: Everything's not lost…

RAVEN 1: Are still in love with Perdita?

RAVEN 3: I put her in my dreams.

RAVEN 1: You're a dream boy.

RAVEN 3: I'm a bird.

RAVEN 1: You're going to fly away if you're not careful, dream boy, Straight into that tree. And down you go.

RAVEN 3: I could still have her. She remembers me.

RAVEN 2: Perdita doesn't remember anybody. She's married now. She's got a position in society. Her lostness is of another variety.

RAVEN 3: She'll come back to me. I see her through my lens.

RAVEN 2: What do you see?

RAVEN 3: She waits for me with open eyes and an open heart. With soft hands that caress me, she tucks me to sleep.

RAVEN 2: Get off that cloud, bird.

RAVEN 3: Better a cloud than concrete.

11.

[Perdita approaches Flori. His eyes are closed.]

PERDITA: Flori? Flori? Are you awake?

FLORI: I am now.

PERDITA: I'm sorry.

FLORI: What is it?

PERDITA: Go back to sleep.

FLORI: What is it?

PERDITA: I missed you, that's all.

FLORI: I'm right here.

PERDITA: I know. But sometimes I miss you even when you're right next to me.

FLORI: Have you been dreaming again?

PERDITA: ...I think our girl is dreaming now.

FLORI: Did you feel a kick?

PERDITA: A little one. Yes. She must be happy.

FLORI: How do you know it will be a girl?

PERDITA: I feel it. Don't you want a girl?

FLORI: Of course. She'll be just like you.

PERDITA: You say that with regret.

FLORI: I can't control the way I say things, Perdita.

PERDITA: …I woke you. I'm sorry.

FLORI: I needed to get up anyway. What time is it?

PERDITA: It's ten years time.

FLORI: What?

PERDITA: It's late.

FLORI: I shouldn't sleep so much. It delays me. I get up and half the day is gone. With all the work I have to do…

PERDITA: It's Sunday.

FLORI: I need to catch up on work for tomorrow. I hate catching up at the office.

PERDITA: Must you do it now?

FLORI: You want to go out, go ahead. You always do.

PERDITA: Are you angry with me?

FLORI: No.

PERDITA: You haven't kissed me yet.

FLORI: Alright. One kiss. *[light kiss]* And now I have to work.

PERDITA: Rules to live by.

FLORI: I've always had them. You just didn't notice.

PERDITA: I notice everything, Flori.

FLORI: Did you notice I'm getting fat?

PERDITA: I love you anyway.

FLORI: You disappear from me. For hours. Where do you go?

PERDITA: Nowhere.

FLORI: I hear things. Rumors. I don't want to believe them because… I don't want to, because we've built a life, and now we'll finally have a child, and I want to believe it is ours.

PERDITA: What are you saying?

FLORI: …I have to work.

PERDITA: Don't bury yourself in work. What's happening with you?

FLORI: My youth is wasting away. Other than that, nothing. Absolutely nothing.

PERDITA: What are you talking about, Flori?

FLORI: Just think about what you do, Perdita, all right? Just think.

[Flori exits.]

PERDITA: Dear child, whisper me a story, from inside my womb. I need your voice, dear child. I need a bright tale for this winter's gloom.

12.

[Mid-res]

FRIP: Name her Gracia.

PERDITA: What's that?

FRIP: It's a Latin name, Spanish or Italian or something. It means grace.

PERDITA: Gracia?

FRIP: I come across it in a book once. The name's stuck with me ever since.

PERDITA: Gracia… …I like it

FRIP: Yeah? Well, keep it in mind. Cause if it's a boy, we'll have to think of something else. Angelus, Angus, something…

[Frip walks away.]

PERDITA: Where are you off to, Frip?

FRIP: I'm going to go bother the fish. Scare off some of the damn tourists. Got to keep moving about in this lost place.

[Frip exits.]

13.

[Perdita is watching television. It is a soap opera. The TV scene is thus played in that style and underscored with emotion-appropriate music cues.]

LEON (mediated): Tell me, Hermione, that you have not slept with him?

HERMIONE (mediated): I tell you true.

LEON (mediated): You lie. Like all women.

HERMIONE (mediated): How long have we been married, Leon? You know me.

LEON (mediated): I have been a fool all this time. Get out of my house. And take your unborn bastard with you.

HERMIONE (mediated): Have you no shame? No memory of what binds us truly?

LEON (mediated): I have seen you looking at him, at my best friend, for God's sake. Do not speak to me of shame when it is you who should have it.

HERMIONE (mediated): If I didn't have your child inside of me, I would strike you.

LEON (mediated): Go on. Do it. And I'll have something else to hold against you.

HERMIONE (mediated): I have only been a good wife to you, Leon. Please, do not do this. You will drive yourself mad with suspicion and there is nothing to suspect. Nothing at all.

LEON (mediated): Lie to me. Go on. Keep lying. The only thing I will accept is your falsehood.

[Flori appears. Screen goes dark as Perdita turns off the TV.]

FLORI: I thought I heard the TV.

PERDITA: I turned it off.

FLORI: You didn't have to.

PERDITA: It's always the same story. Are you all right?

FLORI: I'm fine. Why?

PERDITA: No kiss.

[He kisses her.]

What do you think of the name Gracia?

FLORI: What?

PERDITA: For the baby.

FLORI: It's a name.

PERDITA: Don't you like it?

FLORI: I haven't thought about a name. I've got other things to think about, Perdita.

PERDITA: Frip says it means "grace."

FLORI: Were you talking to him?

PERDITA: He's a good man.

FLORI: He drinks too much. He's not right in the head. They caught him the other night cursing at strangers on the boardwalk.

PERDITA: He was my father's best friend, Flori. He helped raised me.

FLORI: You cling to the past as if it was going to save you.

PERDITA: I'm not clinging to anything. I like talking to him. I asked him to be our baby's godfather.

FLORI: Without asking me?

PERDITA: I thought you wouldn't mind.

FLORI: You don't seem to mind a lot of things. I don't know why the hell I'm here.

PERDITA: What do you mean?

FLORI: Why did we get married, Perdita?

PERDITA: What kind of question...

FLORI: It's a real question. Why did we?

PERDITA: Because we shared the same dream.

FLORI: That's not a good reason. It's not money or privilege, is it? It's not security.

PERDITA: Security is not a reason to get married.

FLORI: Seems like an awfully good one to me. Secure in who you are, in what you want, need from life, secure in money, in what's possible...

PERDITA: What are you thinking?

FLORI: I've heard enough from the men at the office. I've heard plenty. And I'm finally opening my eyes. Screwing around with the ravens. Screwing around with everybody.

PERDITA: Those men at the office are snakes. They're trying to destroy you, and us. They're infecting you with jealousy. Don't let them, please.

FLORI: I don't know what to think about anything. I see you with a baby inside of you, and my mind's all…I risked a lot to marry you. I followed my heart. Like a blind fool. I didn't care what anybody said. And people said things then. My step-dad's friends, my friends… But I was true, right? 'I fell into you like a stone.' There was no one else. And I could've had anyone. That's the truth. I was a real catch. You know? And I'm not bragging. I had a lot of prospects. But I chose you cause I was baffled by you, and intrigued and knew I could give you something you didn't have, which was a concrete sense of things, cause half your mind is in the stars, isn't it? And we've had ten years. And now a child, after trying for so long, and all the headaches and giving up hope and hoping again, and what do I get? I get laughed at at the office. I get smirks and foul jokes. And as much as I try not to listen…

PERDITA: I made a sweater for the baby. Do you like it?

FLORI: I don't know. I don't know anything anymore.

PERDITA: Know you can believe in me.

FLORI: I'm sorry, Perdita. I'm sorry.

[Flori exits. After a moment, Perdita turns on the TV. Screen shows Hermione on the soap opera. She is in mid-sentence.]

HERMIONE (mediated): …to be anything but true, and now you accuse me. You scorn me.

[Perdita lip-synchs to Hermione's speech, which is slowed-down slightly and echoes through the space.]

HERMIONE (mediated)/PERDITA (lip-synch)
Each night I get up and wonder when you will come back to bed, when you will surrender your pride and let go of the lunacy that is inside you. Each night I wait for your caress and there is nothing because you have lost faith in me.

[Screen image suspends.]

14.

[Bosco on an ice floe.]

BOSCO: She is willful and impulsive.
She moves with grace.
She has a secretive smile and endless patience,
This is my love. I have found her.
After years of searching.
I took my boat and pitched it at sea and her
angled eyes woke me.
They said "What are you waiting for, love?"

[AXL appears, transformed as a Mermaid.]

AXL-MERMAID: What are you waiting for,
love?

BOSCO: And I knew it was her.

AXL-MERMAID: In and out of hollers

BOSCO: On the cold ice, in the fresh snow,
along cleft and crease, we met

AXL-MERMAID: In slow orbits.

BOSCO: Mad as kings

AXL-MERMAID: We gave ourselves to each other

BOSCO: High to heaven.

AXL-MERMAID: And I was transformed. I was given shape by your selflessness.
"What are you waiting for, love?" I asked, and you answered

BOSCO: "I'm waiting for you. I've waited all this time for someone to find me."
I didn't care anymore about the island, about anything. This was my time, right? This is what I dreamt: a perfect existence, a lover running with his beloved in the extreme wilderness, outside of the machinations of the whirligig we call life. This is a story for those who lose faith and don't understand the nature of love. See things for what they are and embrace them.

AXL-MERMAID: He saw me for what I was.

BOSCO: A mermaid, a mythical thing.

AXL-MERMAID: Half-human

BOSCO: Half everything.

AXL-MERMAID: And I showed him another planet.

BOSCO: Pre-God, pagan. Nature to nature. At one with the elements.

AXL-MERMAID: I led him.

BOSCO: With a kiss flush on the lips and years of cutting fish behind me. I think of nothing now but her. I have forgotten everything.

[Axl sings:]

"Pale moon (variation)"

AXL-MERMAID
And the pale moon shines at night
Brilliant as a spark of ice
I wander and let you be my guide
Our future is a roll of the dice
Come on, come on, lover
Lead me to redemption, to redemption…
Shed the last trace of your pride.

BOSCO: How can I resist you?

AXL-MERMAID: How can you leave everything behind?

BOSCO: In love, you leave all else for the other thing you seek and you don't question; you follow, because that's all you can do. As soon as you start to question where love begins, how it is you're in it, you're through.

AXL-MERMAID: And for a while we have the same dream.

BOSCO: It is of an island

AXL-MERMAID: Where time has slipped

BOSCO: And torn up the rocks

AXL-MERMAID: And muddied the sand.

BOSCO: But the water is still green.

AXL-MERMAID: In the right light, if you let yourself see it. Yes, it can be.

BOSCO: And that verdant light is about promise

AXL-MERMAID: Possibility.

BOSCO: The future glimpsed

AXL-MERMAID: In a ray of green.

BOSCO: You understand, don't you? You see right through me.

AXL-MERMAID: And what will you give me?

BOSCO: Human-ness, yearning, ache,

AXL-MERMAID: Comfort, silence, words of grace.

BOSCO: The best of me

AXL-MERMAID: Your temper

BOSCO: Un-tempered, curbed, willingly. In the right mood, on a good day, on the flow of ice, I will give you what my mother gave me, which was endless, unconditional, surprising, unswerving love. I have this in me to give. I have this great capacity. The knowledge of it has kept me at bay, un-moored because there was no direction for it, no aim. I see Perdita in your eyes. I try to imagine what her life is like. Is it ruin or glory? Has she found peace? Lost girl, lost heart, too big of a heart and not knowing it. That's the shame, isn't it? To not know your heart.

AXL_MERMAID: Love is a silver thread
Invisible, un-noticed
Until we find it in our dreams.

[Bosco and the transformed Axl kiss.]

15.

[Flori watches Perdita and Raven 3 make love in his mind's eye.]

FLORI: Doubt enters. It fills us up. It burrows deep. The heart is torn by doubt
And there is no stopping it. I try, but the more I do, the more doubt claims its hold on me. I can't look at her now without thinking she's with someone else. I can't touch her without wondering if the child she bears is ours. I am turned inside out. I am ravaged by thoughts and whispers. I punish myself. But punishment serves no purpose when doubt remains. Doubt is a poison. It infects the blood. And once it is in your veins, there is little you can do but give in slowly, and let everything fade. …I say goodbye to her each morning. I kiss her empty pillow and become accustomed to her absence. I am learning how to live without love. This lesson I am teaching myself, so I can go on. Each day it is a little easier. Each day I doubt her more. And one day I will lose her completely. There is nothing I can do. I am consumed. My vision is corrupted. I breathe doubt. I taste it. I hold it

on my tongue. I ask nothing and imagine everything.

16.

[Ravens watch Perdita.]

RAVEN 2: The sad girl looks at her hands.

RAVEN 1: She clutches her womb and worries.

RAVEN 3: Silence enters the strange house
Where desire used to breathe.

[Flori enters.]

FLORI: I saw you the other night.

PERDITA: What do you mean?

FLORI: You were talking to him. You leaned over and kissed him.

PERDITA: I have been here every night.

FLORI: Not last night. You were full of him, weren't you?

PERDITA: There has been no one.

FLORI: No looks?

PERDITA: We all look, Flori. But we don't act on what we see.

FLORI: You stand by the water, you wave, you call to him.

PERDITA: I call to no one. What is the matter with you?

FLORI: "Sweet Flori, delicate Flori…" You were always making me out to be somebody else.

PERDITA: That was years ago.

FLORI: Memories don't leave. They stay, Perdita, right in the brain.

PERDITA: Tell me this is a test of my love, and if it is, all right, I have passed it. I am in love with you. I am steadfast. I am unwavering in your bullying.

FLORI: Are those the words you use with him?

PERDITA: Look at me, Flori.

FLORI: You've lost me, Perdita.

PERDITA: Look at me. …What do you see?

FLORI: The worst of me.

[In the near distance, Frip is seen. He sings:]

"Innocence Ballad"

FRIP
And what do our dreams hold
But what we cannot have
They chill our veins,
Surrender our will
And we give in like fools.

I was innocent once
I was innocent
Long gone now
Long gone.

I was innocent once
I was innocent.
Long gone now.

17.

[Night. Mid-res. Perdita is on the dock's edge. Frip is near her.]

PERDITA: I wish father was here.

FRIP: You miss him.

PERDITA: I think about him every day. I know people say things pass, but they don't. They stay locked inside of you because they're who you are. They're what you're made of. Loss. That's what we're made of. Bits of lost things that find a place inside of us: I don't think I'll be able to go on, Frip.

FRIP: You're ready to die, too?

PERDITA: Flori loves so much he has poisoned himself against me. And I have let him somehow. ...I want to see my baby. That's all I want. I want to hold her in my arms and give her my milk. If I can live long enough to have my child come into this world and have her make a better life for herself, then I'd be happy.

FRIP: You must be cold. We'll take cover.

PERDITA: You believe me, Frip?

FRIP: I believe virtue is overrated. Come on now. Or you'll freeze the life out of you out here.

PERDITA: You're a good person, Frip.

FRIP: I'm a loon, truth be told. Everything inside me is cracked.

18.

[Flori watches television alone in the house. He switches channels. Nothing pleases him. He stops on one channel. It is the soap opera. Hermione speaks. This is a close-up.]

HERMIONE (mediated): Why is your heart so small? What power governs your soul that you can silence yourself to me in this way? I have only been true, my love. That is my weakness. To be constant and true despite all your accusations and doubts and punishments. Look inside yourself *[Hermione is now outside the screen.]* and tell me you do not know this, Flori.

FLORI: What?

HERMIONE : Release your rage, unmask your suspicion. Your child is being born and you do nothing.

FLORI: Damn TV…

HERMIONE : Change every channel you like, Flori. I am on every one of them. Do you hear me? I will torment you until you go to your child and your wife.

FLORI: She screws around with everybody.

HERMIONE : If a woman looks, her eyes do not stray, but return to the gaze of her beloved. If a woman looks elsewhere, seek what is missing in you. Or have you not looked in all these ten years?

FLORI: I'm an honest man.

HERMIONE : Have you not looked elsewhere?

FLORI: No

HERMIONE : Have you not looked elsewhere?

FLORI: Never.

HERMIONE: Look. Look at me. Desire me. Press your lips to mine.

[He does so.]

Want me.

FLORI: I'd do anything.

HERMIONE: Go on, then. Take me.

[He does so.]

FLORI: I don't know what I'm doing.

HERMIONE: You've given up on Perdita.

FLORI: I haven't.

HERMIONE: You've abandoned her.

FLORI: No. I love her. I always have.

HERMIONE: Then why aren't you with her, Flori? Have you not looked, Flori? Have you never looked elsewhere?

FLORI: Yes. But it meant nothing.

[Hermione breaks away from Flori.]

HERMIONE : Shame on you, Flori. Shame. Your child is being born. Your wife is alone. And you do nothing.

[Hermione begins to fade into the screen.]

FLORI: Don't leave. Please. I don't know what…I'm sorry. I'm sorry, Perdita.

[Screen goes dark.]

19.

[Perdita and Flori are illuminated.]

FLORI: In silence, gestures, in small words, in morsels I can relish. Forgive me.

PERDITA: Shut me out, give up on me, release my eyes from yours.

FLORI: Forgive me.

PERDITA: Ask for the impossible.

FLORI: I do.

PERDITA: Ask for it again.

FLORI: I was lost.

PERDITA: I was born lost.

FLORI: I was cursed.

PERDITA: We are all cursed.

FLORI: I wanted you to be someone else, something else, not a part of me.

PERDITA: I wanted to be someone else, somewhere else, not a part of this.

FLORI: …Forgive me.

PERDITA: Forgive me.

FLORI: I arrested you in dreams.

PERDITA: I jailed you in silence.

FLORI: I closed myself up.

PERDITA: And I let you.

FLORI: …Forgive me.

PERDITA: Forgive me.

FLORI: I will be whatever you wish.

PERDITA: Ask for the impossible.

FLORI: I do.

PERDITA: Ask for it again.

FLORI: I will be anything: man, woman, creature, beast

PERDITA: Bird?

FLORI: Yes.

PERDITA: With invisible wings?

FLORI: Yes.

PERDITA: To hold me?

FLORI: Yes.

PERDITA: ……Release me?

FLORI: …Yes. …

20.

[Time passes. Perdita in light. She holds a baby in her arms. Hermione is seen in the distance, watching.]

PERDITA
I named her Grace. Gracia.
I wanted her to have a sense of abundance
right from the start. No trace of lostness.
We've had enough of that.

The island keeps changing.
All the fishermen are gone
and the shops have different names
and even the Green Parrot

is seeing its last days. But it's still home.

Frip took his leave from this world a while ago.
He was a good friend to my father.
 I still call Bosco my father
because there was no one else.
I saw him last summer.
He had a strange woman on his arm.
I could have sworn she had fins.
She looked just like the sea.
I was happy for him. Flori and I tried to work
things out, but…it's hard to forget cruelty.

I'm in a kind of limbo now.
It suits me to be neither one place or another,
with one person or another.
 I have Grace. She's enough. She's everything.
One day I'll reclaim love,
and it'll be quite something.
 I know it. I can just see myself.
 I surf through time, and watch Grace grow
and I think I haven't even started.
 I've got a whole life.

[After slight pause, she sings reprise:]

"Nothing Lost (reprise)"

Dream in the quiet hour
Dream while the light is green
Dream in the brightest hour

Dream while the light is green
Nothing made of nothing lost
Something made of this
Something made of-

[Blackout.]

<u>END OF PLAY</u>

Caridad Svich is a playwright-songwriter-translator and editor of Cuban-Spanish-Argentine-Croatian descent. She is the recipient of New Dramatists' 2007 Whitfield Cook Prize for New Writing for her play *Lucinda Caval*, and the 2003 National Latino Playwriting Award for *Magnificent Waste*. She's also received a Harvard University Radcliffe Institute for Advanced Study Bunting fellowship, a TCG/Pew National Theatre Artist Grant, and has been short-listed twice for the PEN USA-West Award in Drama. Recent premieres: *The Tropic of X* at artheater-Cologne (Germany), her play with alt-country songs *Thrush* at Salvage Vanguard Theatre in Austin, and her US adaptation of the Serbian dark comedy *Huddersfield* as a TUTA production at Victory Gardens Theatre in Chicago, *Iphigenia...a rave fable* at 7 Stages in Atlanta/GA and Son of Semele/CA, her translation of Garcia Lorca's *The House of Bernarda Alba* at the Pearl Theatre/NY, and her multimedia collaboration *The Booth Variations* at 59 East 59th Street Theatre/NY and Edinburgh Fringe Festival/UK. Her free adaptation of Lope de Vega's erotic comedy *The Labyrinth of Desire* premiered at Miracle Theatre in Portland, Oregon spring 2008. **Additional Awards/Residencies:** NEA/TCG Residency at Mark Taper Forum Theatre,

Jonathan R. Reynolds Playwright in Residence
at Denison University; Thurber House Fellow
at Ohio State University; resident playwright at
INTAR Theatre/NY. She has been guest artist
at the Traverse Theatre in Edinburgh, the
Royal Court Theatre, Actors Touring
Company/UK at the Euripides' Festival in
Monodendri, Greece and has taught
playwriting at Yale School of Drama,
Bennington College, Rutgers University, and
the US-Cuba Writers' Conference in Havana.
She is alumna playwright of New Dramatists,
contributing editor of *TheatreForum*, on the
editorial board of *Contemporary Theatre Review*
(Routledge/UK), founder of the national
theatre alliance and publishing press
NoPassport.

Previous key credits: *Alchemy of Desire/Dead-Man's Blues* at the Cincinnati Playhouse in the
Park (winner of the Rosenthal New Play Prize)
under Lisa Peterson's direction, and *Any Place
But Here* at Theater for the New City/NYC
under Maria Irene Fornes' direction. *Fugitive
Pieces* at Cleveland Public Theatre/OH, Kitchen
Dog Theater in Dallas, Texas, and at Salvage
Vanguard in Austin under Jason Neulander's
direction, *The Archaeology of Dreams* at Portland
Stage Company's Little Festival of the
Unexpected, *Twelve Ophelias* was presented at
Baruch Performing Arts Center in New York.
She holds an MFA from UCSD. Her plays and

papers are archived at the University of Miami, Florida and at the Lawrence and Lee Theatre Research Institute at Ohio State University. Her works can be accessed at www.alexanderstreetpress.com, www.lulu.com, and her website is www.caridadsvich.com

Publications: Her translations of Federico Garcia Lorca's work are collected in *Lorca: Six Major Plays* (NoPassport Press) and *Impossible Theater* (Smith & Kraus). Play Publications: *Alchemy of Desire/Dead-Man's Blues* (TCG), *Fugitive Pieces, Luna Park,* and *Any Place But Here* are published by Playscripts Inc. *Prodigal Kiss* and *but there are fires* are published by Smith & Kraus. *Iphigenia...a rave fable* (BackStage Books and *TheatreForum), Twelve Ophelias* (Kendall-Hunt Publishing and *CallReview*), *The Archaeology of Dreams* (Stage & Screen), *Gleaning/Rebusca* (Arte Publico Press), *Scar* (Third Woman Press), *Brazo Gitano (*in *Ollantay Theater Journal).* She is editor of several books on theatre published by Manchester University Press/UK and others.

Lizard Run Press is a boutique imprint
Of NoPassport theatre alliance and press.

NoPassport: Dreaming the Americas

www.ingramcontent.com/pod-product-compliance
Lightning Source LLC
Chambersburg PA
CBHW030322020726
47493CB00004B/1121